Homicide at the Haunted House

NIGHTMARE ARIZONA
PARANORMAL COZY MYSTERIES

BETH DOLGNER

Homicide at the Haunted House

Nightmare, Arizona Paranormal Cozy Mysteries, Book One

© 2023 Beth Dolgner

ISBN-13: 978-1-958587-05-8

Homicide at the Haunted House is a work of fiction. Names, characters, places, and incidents either are the products of the author's imagination or are used fictitiously. Any resemblance to actual persons, living or dead, businesses, companies, events, or locales is entirely coincidental.

Published by Redglare Media
Cover by Dark Mojo Designs
Print Formatting by The Madd Formatter

https://bethdolgner.com

CHAPTER ONE

I crested the hill and squinted as the late-afternoon sun glared through my windshield. Ahead of me, the Interstate stretched in a long, straight line for miles before finally disappearing into a cluster of hills, which were slowly darkening to a purple hue on the horizon.

Red dots danced in my vision, and I blinked, willing my eyes to adjust. No, I realized, it wasn't the sun affecting me. I was seeing brake lights, a whole sea of them about a mile ahead. Beyond them, blue lights flashed. I couldn't see what had happened up there, but I knew it wasn't good.

The three cars in front of me made a last-minute dive onto an exit ramp, and I followed suit. As the Interstate continued down the hill and into the valley, I turned left onto a two-lane road that bridged the Interstate and wound south through the hills. An army of tall Saguaros threw long shadows across the road, and scrubby trees clung desperately to the rocky slopes. Ever since I had crossed the state line into Arizona, the landscape had become increasingly desolate. Everywhere I looked, there was a different kind of cactus waiting to stab me.

I sure hoped the drivers ahead of me knew where they were going. Their cars looked shiny and relatively new, which meant they probably had GPS. My car was so old it only had a radio and a CD player, and I hadn't owned any CDs for at least a decade. That meant I had been listening to local radio stations for the past two days and five states. The last time I knew so many Top 40 songs, I was in college and a full three dress sizes slimmer.

I didn't even have a cell phone anymore, so I couldn't use the map on that. With that thought, I pressed the gas pedal just a little harder to close the small gap between me and the car ahead. There was no way I was going to risk losing sight of them on this winding road. I needed to be able to find my way back onto the Interstate so I could finish up what had to be the most miserable road trip of my life. Just five more hours, and I would be at my brother's house in San Diego. Even if I stopped for some cheap gas station coffee, I would still make it there before midnight.

There were no crossroads as I continued to follow the other cars south. The road was slowly gaining elevation, but it definitely wasn't curving west at all. We were going farther and farther away from the Interstate.

I had been driving on the road for at least twenty minutes when I saw another blinking light. This time, it wasn't from brake lights or police cars. It was the yellow "check engine" light on my dash.

"Oh, come on," I moaned. My eyes darted across the dash, and I watched as the needle on the engine temperature gauge slowly moved upward. "No, no, no. Please, no. I need to get to San Diego tonight!"

Here's the thing about talking to your car: it doesn't talk back, and it definitely does not listen.

Finally, I saw a stop sign coming up. The cars ahead of me were all turning right, going west again to parallel the Interstate. When it was my turn at the intersection, I glanced right and saw nothing but more sharp plants and rocks. I looked straight ahead and saw a plywood sign with faded blue paint that read, *Repairs! Oil Changes! A/C Coolant! 3 Miles Ahead!*

I jumped at the sound of honking, and I glanced in my rearview mirror to see a line of cars snaking behind me, all waiting for their turn to get back to civilization, too. I looked at my dash hopefully, but the engine temperature needle was still rotating toward the top of the gauge, creeping closer to the red "don't you dare keep driving" part.

I sighed, switched off my turn signal, and went straight.

"Only three miles, car," I said coaxingly. "You can do this."

It couldn't. I had only gone about a mile and a half when the dash suddenly lit up like a Christmas tree. The temperature needle was buried in the red. I lost count of the expletives I muttered as I guided the car onto the narrow shoulder and turned it off. I was on a steep incline, so I pulled the parking brake and hoped the car would stay put.

Actually, part of me hoped it would roll off the side of the hill, catch on fire, and explode on contact with the rocky valley below, but then I'd really be stranded.

I figured there was no point trying to take any of my belongings with me. The little I had left to call my own would probably be safe out there; I hadn't passed a single car since I had gone straight through that stop sign. I grabbed my purse, locked up the car, and started walking.

As I hoofed it up the incline, I noticed there were fewer cacti but quite a few taller, leafier trees dotting the landscape. It seemed that the higher I climbed into the hills, the less threatening the plants were. It wasn't much of a silver lining, but it was all I had.

It was hot out, probably one hundred degrees or more, but at least the sun was sinking fast. By the time I finally spotted a whitewashed cinder block garage around a curve in the road, the sun had just sunk beneath the hills on the horizon.

The same faded blue paint I had seen on the plywood sign was also on the side of the garage, with *Done Right Auto Repair* written in a flowing script. By the time I walked through the creaking wooden door at the front of the garage, I was sweaty, tired, and fighting the urge to just start yelling. It wasn't that I was mad at anyone, I was just fed up with the whole situation.

"Be right with you!" The man's voice echoed from a room behind the front office, and soon, the body it belonged to appeared in the doorway. He somehow looked like the garage itself. His oil-streaked white overalls seemed too large on his lean frame, and his blue eyes were as faded as the paint on the sign. He smiled, his teeth bright in contrast to his tanned face. "Good timing. I was just closing up for the weekend. What can I do for you?"

"For the weekend?" I repeated. I brushed a sweaty lock of auburn hair out of my eyes.

"Yeah, I take weekends off so I can spend more time with my daughter." The man gave me a quick wink. "Unless, of course, it's an emergency."

I waved vaguely in the direction I had come from. "My car overheated. I had to ditch it on the side of the road."

The man nodded grimly. "That is an emergency. Let's get your car towed up here, then we'll figure out what's next. I'm Nick Dalton."

"Olivia Kendrick. Thanks." Nick pulled a rag with even more oil and dirt on it than his overalls out of a pocket. He wiped his hand on it before reaching out. I tried to keep my grimace to a minimum as I shook his proffered hand, since I had no interest in being covered in oil, too. Nick's grip was warm and firm, and I was surprised to feel my lips start to turn up into a genuine smile. There was just something comforting about him. *I might be stranded in the middle of nowhere*, I thought, *but at least I'm stranded with this guy.*

In just a few minutes, I was sitting uncomfortably in the passenger seat of Nick's tow truck. The springs sagged, and a rip in the faux-leather upholstery had been covered up with silver duct tape that squeaked every time I shifted. Nick asked me a steady stream of questions as we drove, like where I was headed, where I had come from, and how I had managed to stray so far from the Interstate.

When we pulled up next to my car and came to a stop, Nick whistled. "You came all the way from Nashville in that?" He sounded both horrified and impressed.

"It's all I could afford," I said stiffly, shrugging.

Nick looked at me keenly. "I just didn't think someone carrying such an expensive designer purse would drive a hunk of junk like that."

Ouch. I made a mental note that even though Nick looked like a mess, his mind was sharp. I instinctively clutched my purse closer. When I had sold everything off, I had flat-out refused to get rid of my purse. Some things were nonnegotiable.

It was nearly dark already, and Nick grabbed a big silver flashlight from a box that sat between the driver and passenger seats. "Let's see what we're dealing with," he said before sliding deftly out of the tow truck.

I got out a lot less gracefully, scrambling my way down. Nick was already opening the hood of my car, though, so at least he hadn't witnessed my awkward exit. I walked over to him, and my eyes followed the beam of his flashlight, which he trained at my radiator. I crossed my arms and tried to look like I understood what I was seeing.

Nick suddenly dropped onto his knees to peer underneath the car. He stood up again, produced that same dirty rag, and pulled the dipstick out of the oil reservoir. I suppressed a sardonic laugh. The last car I'd owned hadn't even had a dipstick for checking oil. The car's computer would simply know if the oil was low and beam a message to the dash to tell me it needed service.

"I hate to say it, but you've got an oil leak," Nick said. To his credit, he actually did sound sorry about giving me such bad news. "I had hoped you just needed to top off your radiator fluid, but it's going to take more than that." Nick turned to me with a sympathetic expression. "Even if I order the parts first thing in the morning, they won't arrive until Monday or Tuesday. We don't have that same-day service like in the big cities."

I bit my lip as I quickly and silently did the math in my head. Repairs to the oil system on my car plus at least three nights in a motel were going to add up fast.

Nick seemed to know what I was thinking, because he grinned at me. "Luckily, my parents own a local motel, and they're always happy to give a discount to my customers."

I nodded. My only other choice was to ask if there was a couch at the garage I could crash on.

Nick got my car hooked up to his tow truck, and we made the short drive back to his garage. Once he unhooked my car, I unloaded my two suitcases of clothes, leaving my few boxes of keepsakes in the trunk. I wouldn't need those in the motel.

The drive to the motel was a cramped one. I had expected Nick to have a normal car, but we climbed into the tow truck again. Nick had managed to wedge one of my suitcases behind the seats, but the other was balanced half on my lap and half on the box between us. Every time we hit a bump, I worried the suitcase would knock into Nick's arm and send us careening off the road.

We only drove about a mile before I started seeing a few houses and side streets. We passed a building with several shops in it, and then we rounded a curve, and I found myself looking at a sleepy little town. I couldn't see much in the dark, but the soft yellow streetlights stretched across a relatively flat space dotted with low buildings.

A neon sign blinked on the left-hand side of the road. Green letters reading *Cowboy's Corral Motor Lodge* were topped by a yellow cowboy hat. "Here we are," Nick said proudly.

The motel itself looked as mid-century kitsch as the neon sign. It was made of white cinder block, like the garage, and it had two wings that ran straight back from the street, with parking spaces in between them. At the front of the motel, centered between the driveways that led in and out of the parking area, there was a small, two-story building with neon signs in the front windows that read *Office* and *Satellite TV!*

Nick pulled up right in front of the office. He had already climbed out and unloaded both of my suitcases by the time I had made it out of the passenger side. If I was going to be riding around town with him, I would really have to work on my exit skills.

Nick opened the glass front door of the office, then ushered me into a room with a thick brown carpet and a front desk made of Formica. The woman behind the counter had a grin that was identical to Nick's, and she spread her plump arms in a welcoming gesture. "Welcome to Nightmare, Arizona!"

CHAPTER TWO

"Mama, Olivia here broke down on her way to San Diego," Nick said, nodding at me. "She's going to be here until at least Monday, so can you please give her the friends and family discount?"

"Olivia, is it? I'm Sue Dalton, but a lot of folks just call me Mama." Mama reached out her hand, and I shook it without a second thought: her hands, unlike her son's, were clean. She gave me an exaggerated wink. "It's short for Motor Lodge Mama. Me and Benny have been running this place for almost thirty years now."

"Well, I sure appreciate the discount," I said. "I hadn't budgeted for a weekend in... Did you say this town is called Nightmare?"

"It sure is." Mama smiled proudly. "A lot of these old mining towns out West have funny names. Tombstone, Brilliant, that sort of thing. Life out here wasn't easy for those early settlers, so they had to have a sense of humor!"

Nick gave me a firm clap on the shoulder. "You're in good hands, so I'm heading home. Mama, I'll talk to you tomorrow! Olivia, I'll call you here at the motel as soon as I have anything to say about your car."

I glanced at my white blouse to make sure Nick hadn't left an oil stain on it before I thanked him.

"That's going to be one hundred seven dollars and

twenty-six cents," Mama said as the bell on the office door tinkled.

In my previous life, that would have seemed cheap for one night, let alone three. Now, it seemed steep. I pulled out my wallet and carefully counted out cash for her. I handed her six twenty-dollar bills, all slipped to me by friends when I had said goodbye and left Nashville. It had been touching and humiliating all at the same time.

Mama counted out my change and handed me a key with a blue plastic key chain dangling from it. "You'll be in room thirteen," she said. "It's a lucky number around here, and it seems like you could use a little luck. Just pull around—sorry, I mean, just walk about halfway back, and it will be on the right-hand side, on the ground floor."

I thanked Mama and followed her directions, the wheels on my two suitcases sounding loud as they rolled across the asphalt parking lot. I found my room easily enough, and soon, I was sprawled on top of a brown bedspread that covered a double bed. The room was a little old and shabby, but it was clean. The floor lamp in the corner had a brown and orange floral pattern on the shade, and the carpet was a coordinating shade of orange. I was sure it had looked great in the sixties or seventies, when those colors were popular.

The thin curtains on the front window couldn't completely block the glow of the neon sign, and its incessant blinking finally got me up and moving. It was time to do some accounting. There was a chance I'd have to stay there more than three nights, and there would be the car repairs to pay for.

Plus, I needed money for food. That was an important one.

In just a few minutes, I had a sad small pile of cash and some loose change spread out on the round table that sat in front of the window. I didn't have credit cards anymore, or even a bank account, so this was it.

I was broke.

I spared a moment to think mean, horrible things about my ex-husband, who was the reason I was in this situation right now. If he hadn't wasted all of our savings, then broke the news to me in the same conversation where he asked for a divorce, I wouldn't be stuck in a town called Nightmare. Talk about ironic.

Briefly, I considered calling my brother to ask him for help. Maybe, I thought, he could wire me some money. But I quickly pushed that idea out of my head. He and my sister-in-law were already going above and beyond by letting me stay in their basement guest suite while I tried to start a new life, and asking for even more seemed selfish. Also, it just hurt my pride.

"I can do this," I told myself. I didn't sound very convincing, so I pressed my palms flat on the table and said in a stronger voice, "I can do this!" I had scraped by in my early twenties, when I worked part-time as a server while finishing up college. If I could do it back then, why couldn't I do it now that I was in my early forties? This time, at least, I had twenty extra years of life experience to help me figure it all out.

I needed a job. That was all there was to it. There had to be some kind of temporary work available immediately, and I could stick around a little longer until I got that first paycheck. Then, I would be out of this town and back on the way to my fresh start.

The next morning, I wandered up to the front office to ask Mama where I might be able to find a job. I was happy to see a carafe of coffee sitting on a side table. I hadn't noticed it the night before, but after a restless eight hours filled with nightmares about being stuck in Nightmare, I eagerly grabbed a Styrofoam cup and started pouring.

"I see you have your priorities in order," I heard Mama call from behind the Formica counter.

I turned to see her smiling at me. "Good morning. And yes, I need a cup before I head out on a mission." I walked over and leaned my elbows on the counter. "I need to find a job. Preferably something in marketing, like I used to do in Nashville, but I'll take whatever I can get."

Mama's eyebrows shot up in surprise above her bright-blue eyes, but just as quickly, her expression returned to a neutral one. "Oh, you plan to stay awhile? I thought you were on your way somewhere else and just so happened to break down here."

"Well," I said, averting my gaze. I hastily took a sip of coffee, but it was too hot, and I sputtered as the liquid scalded my tongue. It didn't taste good. It was weak and slightly burnt, but I reminded myself it was free.

When I glanced up again, there was something like sympathy in Mama's eyes, but her tone was all business. "There's a community job board you can check. It might be a little bare, though. Tourist season won't start until we get into the fall, when the weather finally cools down, so a lot of the seasonal jobs aren't available yet."

"Tourist season? You mean people come here—" I cut myself off before I could say "on purpose." Instead, I continued, "For sightseeing?"

"Oh, yeah." Mama straightened her shoulders and gave her fluffy, wavy gray hair a proud pat. "Nightmare was a copper mining town back in the late 1800s. When the mine went bust, this place practically became a ghost town. Then artists started showing up, taking advantage of the cheap real estate for their homes and studios. After that, folks who like catering to tourists came along, offering mine tours, sprucing up the grand old hotel, and the like. We're a thriving tourist town now."

Mama gave me directions to the job board and

promised it was only a ten-minute walk from the motel. Even in my khaki shorts and blue tank top, I figured I'd be a sweaty mess by the time I got there. It was shaping up to be another hot day.

I turned left out of the motel and walked past a row of old wooden houses and a few small adobe buildings that housed businesses. Ahead, there was a higher concentration of buildings, which Mama had referred to as "downtown." It hardly qualified as a town at all, in my opinion.

There was a steady stream of cars coming down the road and turning a short way ahead of me, and I realized they were going to the same place I was. Mama had told me to turn right at the coyote statue, promising I wouldn't need to know the street name. She was right: the giant statue looked like it was made of plaster, and it was painted an eye-watering shade of yellow. Behind it, a squat building with no windows had a sign reading, *The Neon Coyote*. It appeared to be a biker bar, and even though it wasn't even lunchtime yet, there were already a few bikes parked out front.

I crossed the road and walked one block, then made a left as Mama had instructed. I was only one street back from the main road, but it felt like an entirely different world. No, I realized, not a different world. A different time. Here, the street had been covered in dirt, and the wooden buildings looked like something from a Wild West movie set.

I stepped onto the covered boardwalk that lined the street, but before I could continue, I saw a blur of movement as someone jumped in front of me. A black-and-white flyer was suddenly inches from my face, and I yelped.

"Have you seen them?" said a voice. I couldn't even see the man holding the flyer, let alone "them."

I reached up and grabbed the bottom of the flyer, pulling it gently downward. The man was dressed in jeans and a black T-shirt, which had a graphic of a cow being beamed up into a saucer-shaped UFO. His graying brown hair was slightly wild, and his hazel eyes bulged.

"They've been here before, and not for the last time!" The man's voice was shaking with excitement.

"Who?" I asked. Part of me wanted to brush past this guy, but a part of me was also curious.

"The visitors."

"You mean the tourists?"

The man laughed incredulously. "No! The visitors from across the galaxy. Come join our watch party at Barker Ranch on Friday night!" He shoved the flyer toward me again, and I instinctively curled my fingers around it before it could fall to the ground.

I nodded as politely as I could, then sidestepped him and kept walking. *I guess every town has its weirdos.*

I passed a shop called The General Store, though it looked to me like it was mostly stocked with souvenirs. Across the street, an old wooden building with a high front facade and a balcony on the second story had a sign advertising a can-can dancing show.

This part of Nightmare was something else. Even though the boardwalks were crowded with people who were obviously as modern as me, I still half expected to see a cowboy in a duster with a gun strapped to his hip.

No sooner had I thought that, than I spotted a cowboy in a black duster and matching hat walking right toward me. As he got closer, I saw him reach down and twitch one side of his duster away from his body. His fingers curled around the gun strapped to his hip.

"You got a lot of nerve, coming to this town!" the cowboy shouted.

He was looking right at me, and I froze. Just as I was bringing a finger up to point at myself in a *Who, me?*

gesture, I heard another man's voice directly behind me. "You don't own this town, McCrory."

I whirled around and found myself face-to-face with a guy who looked like he ought to be robbing a stagecoach. He was even wearing a red bandanna over his nose and mouth.

The first cowboy took another step in my direction, and I jumped out of the way. "No, but you're not welcome here, all the same, Tanner."

The one called Tanner produced his own gun, and I turned and pressed my back up against the wall of the general store as hard as I could. First aliens, and now a shootout? What kind of a town was Nightmare?

CHAPTER THREE

I glanced at a group of people standing right behind McCrory. Why weren't they running for cover?

Because, I realized, they were too busy holding up cameras and cell phones. I felt myself relax as I realized this was a staged gunfight put on by actors. At the same time, I could feel my cheeks burning in embarrassment. How could I have not realized it was just a show for tourists?

It's because you've been under a lot of stress and going through big upheavals lately, Olivia, I told myself. *You've got hair-trigger emotions.*

And speaking of triggers, the cowboys were still trading barbs as they began to move into the dusty street. I dodged the people hurrying past me along the boardwalk to catch the show. I had already made it onto the next block before I heard the distinct *pop-pop* of the cowboys' cap guns.

The job board was just where Mama had told me it would be. The dirty old corkboard was hung next to the door of the Nightmare Chamber of Commerce. A small pewter plaque below the board informed me the building had been the Nightmare Central Bank from 1882 to 1910, closing shortly after the copper mine had stopped giving up quality ore.

I had been prepared for a dismal selection of jobs, but

the reality was even worse than I had imagined. There were only seven jobs posted. Two of them were clearly weeks, if not months, old, judging by their dirty, slightly mangled looks. Three of the other so-called jobs were for things that sounded vaguely like pyramid schemes.

That left just two options for me. One of them started out promising, offering four hundred dollars a week in cash. I sucked in my breath hopefully, then quickly let it all out in a sigh as I continued to read that the position was for welding work.

The final job listing was handwritten on a small piece of textured paper, not printed off a computer like all the rest. The script was slanted, and the letters were sharply pointed, giving the words a vaguely urgent, excited feel.

The first line read *Nightmare Sanctuary Haunted House*. I almost gave up and turned away right then and there, but I persevered. The ad went on to read, *Arizona's most popular year-round haunted attraction needs YOU! Get full-time pay for part-time work, paid weekly in cash... that is, if you're not too scared!*

There was a phone number following that and nothing more. No details about the job itself, what it really paid, or even whether some kind of qualifications would be required for the position. If I needed some sort of skills, I would be out of luck: I had been to exactly two haunted houses back when I was a teenager, and I had kept my eyes shut and my hands clamped over my ears through both. Not exactly real-world experience.

Still, I was enticed by the idea of full-time pay for part-time hours, and I was even more excited about the idea of being paid weekly. Maybe I would only need the job for a week or two, and then I could pay for the car and the motel, and still have enough gas money to make it to San Diego.

I didn't have a pen in my purse to write down the number. I'd stopped carrying one because I was used to simply using my cell phone to take a photo or type notes, and when I had given up my phone, I hadn't immediately reverted to my old-fashioned ways.

My only other option was to take the ad with me. I felt a little bad about that, since it meant other job-seekers wouldn't see the opportunity. But, I told myself while pulling the pushpin out of the corkboard, less competition would give me a better chance of getting the position.

I slid the piece of paper into my purse. I hadn't noticed if my time-capsule motel room had a phone in it, but I was sure Mama would let me use the one at the front desk to call about the job. Just as I turned and looked out at the Wild West street, feeling slightly less judgmental about it now that I had a job prospect, my stomach gave a loud rumble. I clamped a hand over my belly and looked around to make sure no one else had heard it. I had been so focused on job-hunting I hadn't stopped to think about eating, but I suddenly realized I was starving. I hadn't eaten dinner the night before, since I had been too busy dealing with my broken-down car. This morning, I had been grateful simply to get a free cup of coffee, even if it had been burnt.

I could only afford about ten dollars a day for food. Although, if I got this job at the haunted house, maybe I could bump it up by a few bucks. In the meantime, though, I was on a tight budget. I hadn't spotted a single sign for a fast-food restaurant out on the main street, so I turned and walked into the Chamber of Commerce.

A man with a thick mustache and wire-rimmed glasses greeted me with a loud, "Howdy!" I wondered if he sometimes played McCrory, Tanner, or some other old-time cowboy.

"Good morning," I said, absolutely unable to match his level of enthusiasm. "I'm looking for somewhere around here to get lunch. Ah, somewhere inexpensive." I lowered my eyes. "I'm a little tight on cash at the moment."

I spared another, albeit brief, moment to think mean things about my ex. I used to drive a German sports car and get my nails done every week. Now, I was asking about the cheapest eats in a town called Nightmare.

The man pointed in the opposite direction of the main road. "You want to go to The Lusty Lunch Counter. Go over three streets, then turn left and walk about half a block." The man's eyes narrowed as he peered at me. "You new in town?"

I glanced down at myself. Was I that obvious? "Yeah, I just got here last night."

"Uh-huh. I thought so. Here's a tip: this street here is High Noon Boulevard, and it's tourist pricing from one end to the other. The local folks know not to waste their money here. Things get a lot more affordable the second you step off this street, but the Lusty is definitely the cheapest."

I thanked the man and turned to leave, then paused. Since this was the Chamber of Commerce, what better place to enquire about a local business? "What can you tell me about Nightmare Sanctuary Haunted House?"

The man shrugged, but I noticed the way his eyes slid away from mine and focused on the wall next to us. "That place brings a lot of folks into our town, so the motels and shops and restaurants all benefit."

"But?" I prompted.

He shrugged again. "Some strange folks over there. Not bad ones, mind you, just strange. Though, I guess a haunted house isn't exactly a place where normal people work."

Except, maybe, for people like me, who are absolutely desperate for money.

"Gotcha. Thanks again for your help." I gave the man a wave and set out to quiet my rumbling stomach.

The Lusty Lunch Counter was exactly where the guy at the Chamber of Commerce had told me it would be. It was in a two-story clapboard building whose paint had long since worn off, leaving just the bare wood, which had faded to a gray color. Like many of the buildings I had seen on High Noon Boulevard, this one had the tall false front that made the building appear much higher than it actually was. The balcony looked slightly tilted, but I spied a few diners sitting at the tables out there, seemingly unconcerned for their safety.

Inside, the restaurant looked a lot more, well, modern wasn't the word, but it was definitely not trying to give off an old mining town vibe. Bright overhead lights shined down onto two rows of booths with overstuffed red seating and a long counter with a gleaming stainless-steel surface.

I had barely settled onto an empty stool at the counter when a menu was put down in front of me. A server with a high ponytail and big hoop earrings was already whipping out a pen and an order pad. "Hi, hon, what can I get you to drink?"

I ordered a water and began to peruse the menu to see what would get me the biggest bang for my buck. My eyes landed on the lunch special—a cheeseburger and fries—for six dollars. With tax and tip, I would be a hair under my daily budget. One meal was all I was going to get today, so I sure hoped it was a big pile of fries.

I ordered when the server returned with my water, then I leaned forward and asked, "What's with the name of this place, anyway?"

"Oh, you're new here, huh? This building was the home of the best brothel in Nightmare." She flashed me a wicked smile before turning away.

How was I even supposed to react to that? Not only

was I eating in a place that used to be a brothel, but the fact it had been the best one in Nightmare implied there had been more than one. I vaguely wondered if the haunted house was in one of the others. Getting scared in a former house of ill repute seemed less strange than eating in one. It also seemed more sanitary.

As I waited for my food, I gazed around the diner, since I didn't have a cell phone to scroll through or any other kind of distraction. It wasn't long before a voice began to intrude on my thoughts. It was a man's voice, and even though I could tell he was trying to keep his volume down, his angry tone still carried over to where I was sitting. I turned slightly on my stool and looked out of the corner of my eye to see two men seated at the booth directly behind me. A man in a suit sat on one side, and on the other was a man wearing a plaid Western shirt.

"Are you kidding me?" hissed the one in the suit. "How can you possibly turn that down?"

"It's not about the money," drawled his companion. He didn't seem angry at all. Rather, he seemed bored, and maybe a little annoyed.

"Then what is it about?" continued the first man. "What's the whole point of all those years of work if you can't cash in someday? You say yes, and you'll be retired in a month!"

Mr. Plaid Shirt mumbled something that I couldn't hear.

"You have to reconsider."

I stopped pretending that I wasn't eavesdropping and gave the pair my full attention as the one in the plaid shirt stood up abruptly. He was well built, and his tanned skin and tousled dark-blond hair gave him a distinctly rugged look.

He could give the country boys in Nashville a run for their money.

20

"Please. All you have to do is sign some paperwork," said the man in the suit. He looked up pleadingly.

Plaid Shirt leaned forward and rested his hands on the table, his face close to his companion's. "Over my dead body."

CHAPTER FOUR

I watched as the guy in the plaid shirt stalked out of the diner. It was only the *plunk* of a plate being dropped in front of me that snapped my eyes away from the scene. As I turned to find the generous portion of french fries I had hoped for, I considered that what I had just witnessed had been another staged fight, like the one I had seen between the two cowboys. But, no, of course not, I told myself. This was a place for locals. That had been real drama. It was like getting dinner and a show, but on a budget.

By the time I was done eating, the man in the suit had left, too. I walked back to the motel, taking a route that bypassed the tourist street. I wanted the quieter environment as I revved myself up for calling about the job at the haunted house.

I was hot, sweaty, and dusty by the time I got back to my motel room, but at least I had a full belly. There was, in fact, a phone in my room, sitting on the nightstand. I pulled the job listing for the haunted house out of my purse and perched on the edge of the bed. I took three deep breaths before I picked up the phone and started dialing. The process actually relaxed me a little bit, since I was so distracted by having to use a rotary phone. I was sure there were a lot of people younger than me who wouldn't even know how to make a call with a phone like that.

A woman answered the phone on the third ring. Her voice had a crisp, slightly harried tone. "Nightmare Sanctuary, can I help you?"

"Hello, I'm calling about your open position."

There was a pause, and when the woman spoke again, her pace was slower, clearer. "This is Nightmare Sanctuary Haunted House."

"Yes, I know. I saw your post on the community job board outside the Chamber of Commerce, and I was calling to see if the position is still open."

"When did you see the post?"

"Just this morning." *And why,* I asked myself, *does that even matter?*

"Um… Can you please hold for a moment?"

Before I could even say yes, I heard a *click*, followed by quiet orchestral music that sounded like it should be playing over video footage of a cemetery at midnight. At least the place had appropriate on-hold music.

It was a full three minutes before the voice on the other end of the line came back. I knew exactly how long it was, since I desperately needed a job so I could keep eating cheap cheeseburgers, and every second felt like an hour. The woman had sounded a little stressed when she had originally answered the phone, but when she spoke again, her tone had changed to one that sounded curious. "Can you come in this afternoon for an interview? Maybe around three thirty?"

"Yes, thank you! I'll see you then." I hung up before I realized I hadn't even asked for her name. I had no idea where to go when I got there, let alone whom to talk to. I also had zero idea what I was supposed to wear to an interview for a job at a haunted house. I know they say to dress for the job you want, but I wasn't going to roll in there looking like a ghoul.

In the end, I opted for black trousers, a knit blouse with

an orange and yellow floral print, and black wedges. The shoes looked professional but would still be comfortable enough for walking all the way to my interview. As for the rest of the outfit, well, I figured the orange and black gave me a bit of a Halloween look, at least.

I left my room plenty early so I could stop by the front office. Mama was just handing a room key over to a smiling young couple, and I expected the convertible parked out front must be theirs. I envied their nice car and road-trip enthusiasm. As soon as they were done at the counter, I stepped up.

"You look like you're going to apply for a job," Mama noted. "That was quick!"

"Yeah! I have an interview at Nightmare Sanctuary Haunted House. I was wondering if you could please give me directions there?"

Mama's face clouded over. "Nightmare Sanctuary? You sure you want to work at that place?"

I nervously ran a hand through my shoulder-length hair. "Why not?"

Mama gave a judgmental sniff. "There are some weird folks working at that place. That's all I'm saying."

It was just what the man at the Chamber of Commerce had told me, and I felt my shoulders sag. If the employees had that bad of a reputation, maybe I didn't want this job.

Then again, I could put up with just about anything for a week or two. It was all about getting me out of this town and back on the road to San Diego.

Mama gave me directions that didn't involve any coyote statues this time, but she did tell me to turn right at the gallows, adding there was no way I could miss that landmark. Nightmare Sanctuary was about a mile from the motel, but she assured me there would be some shade along the route, so I shouldn't be too much of a soggy mess by the time I got there.

I set out feeling like that morning's cup of coffee had just kicked in. I was practically vibrating between my desperation for a job, my nervousness about the people I was about to encounter, and my feeling of being squeezed between a very hot rock and a hard place.

Instead of turning left onto the main road, like I had done to reach High Noon Boulevard, I turned right and crossed the road at the next intersection. The little street I found myself walking down was lined with grand, if dilapidated, Victorian houses. The houses became less frequent as I continued, and after about half a mile, I was walking under massive pecan trees that lined the road. The shade and a light breeze kept me cool, and I slowed my pace. I still had plenty of time, and there was no need to hustle.

The line of trees ended abruptly at a crossroads. The gallows Mama had mentioned stood ominously at the opposite corner from me. It felt like some kind of warning. I gaped at them for only a moment before I turned right onto a dirt road with low trees crowding up against its sides. The road wound lazily up a hill, and when I reached the crest, I stopped and gasped at the scene in front of me.

A massive stone building sat in a hollow space between the hills, surrounded by a garden that managed to be both overgrown and dead at the same time. Thick weeds marched right up to the foundation of the building, which was four stories tall. It looked far more ominous than the gallows had.

The road I was on ran down the hill and curved left, ending at a massive grassy field that I figured doubled as a parking lot. I followed the road until I was standing right in front of the building. An old circular drive made of flagstones was nearly obscured by weeds, and in the middle of the drive's arc, a large, black sign had blood-red letters reading *Nightmare Sanctuary Haunted House*. Below the sign was a pile of huge iron cogs, rusted old bins, and something that looked vaguely like a drill made for a giant. I figured it was leftover equipment from the old copper mine.

Unlike the overgrown drive, the stone walkway that led to the entrance of the building was well maintained, and a smaller walk fed into it from the parking lot. As I got closer to the building, I could see words engraved into the stone over the high, arched front doors: *Nightmare Sanctuary Hospital and Asylum.*

A little shudder worked its way up my back. People used to come to this creepy place to be healed? It seemed like just seeing this building would make anyone feel worse. I could only hope it had been a prettier, more inviting spot back when it was a hospital, when the gardens were still tended, and the stone hadn't yet become darkened and stained with time.

The double front doors were set slightly back from the front of the building, creating a covered portico. As I entered its shade and headed for the doors, I heard a voice rumble, "We're not open yet."

I jumped. I was letting the place get to me already. I turned to see a door and an open window on my right-hand side. The window had been fitted with a narrow countertop. A sign told me this was the ticket window, and the surly-looking man standing in its open space didn't look happy to see me. He had high cheekbones topped by large, dark-brown eyes, which seemed especially dark compared to his pale skin. His thick rust-red hair flowed down over his shoulders. I cautiously took a step forward and plastered a polite smile onto my face as I fought my sudden discomfort. There was something almost wild about the man.

"I'm here for a job interview," I said timidly.

The man didn't answer. Instead, he just leaned over the ticket counter and stared at me.

"It's at three thirty," I prompted.

"I know." He disappeared from the window, and a second later, the door opened, and he stepped out. I could see how muscular his legs were under his tight, faded jeans. "Come on."

The man didn't say another word to me as he opened one of the front doors and ushered me into a spacious entryway with a high ceiling. It looked like something I would expect to see in a castle in England, not in an old mining town hospital. We turned right just inside the doors and went down a hallway. The man stopped at an open door about halfway down on our left, said, "She's here," then turned and brushed past me on his way back out.

"Come in." The voice was clearly the same one I had heard on the phone, and I braced myself for whatever the body belonging to it might look like. Or feel like: I'm not into woo-woo stuff, but that ticket-taker had been giving off some negative energy, for sure.

I nearly sighed in relief when I walked into the room. It looked like an office, albeit one that appeared to have been decorated about a century ago. Behind a massive oak desk sat a totally normal-looking woman with wavy chestnut hair pulled back with barrettes. She stood and came around the desk, her tall form moving quickly and gracefully.

"I'm Justine Abbott," she said, smiling and extending a hand. "My apologies for whatever rude behavior you saw from Zach. He's only in a good mood about three days a month."

"Olivia Kendrick," I said, shaking Justine's hand. Her green eyes shone in her round face, and I decided right then and there that I liked her. There might be weird characters at Nightmare Sanctuary, like Zach, but Justine seemed all right.

Justine gestured to an oxblood leather chair in front of the desk as she returned to her spot. "Sit, please. Did you bring a resume?"

"Oh!" I went from feeling at ease to totally flustered in the span of half a second. "No, I didn't even think of it. I'm so sorry. How unprofessional of me."

"It's okay," Justine assured me. "You can see what a mess I've got here." She gestured to the mountains of papers piled up on the desk. "Our owner is... not here right now, so I'm filling in as director. It's a bit chaotic, so even if you did have a resume, I'd probably just lose it. So, tell me, what did you do prior to this?"

"I worked for a marketing firm in Nashville."

"What brought you all the way out to Nightmare?"

Oh, boy. I was going to have to word this carefully. I could feel sweat beading on my forehead. I couldn't just tell her the truth, of course. Instead, I stammered, "I just got divorced, and I'm trying to get a fresh start."

Okay, so I had told her the truth. I just left out the part where I mentioned that Nightmare was only a pit stop on the way to my new life.

"What made you choose this job to apply for, as opposed to the other listings?" Justine sat back in her chair and laced her fingers together in her lap.

I laughed nervously. "Honestly? It was the only one that wasn't a pyramid scheme or something I have zero qualifications for."

Justine cocked her head ever so slightly, and I felt like she was scrutinizing me. "Okay. Well, if you aren't opposed to working at night and sometimes being in dark spaces, then I'm happy to offer the job to you."

"Great! What—"

"But!" Justine leaned forward. "You should experience

Nightmare Sanctuary before you commit. Come back tonight, and there will be two tickets waiting for you at the window."

That was a little different than just filling out an application, but I could see the logic in experiencing the haunted house before starting to actually work there. I agreed and asked what kind of work the position entailed.

Justine rose and gestured to me to follow her. She walked me down the hall toward the front door as she said vaguely, "Oh, a little of everything. Selling tickets, monitoring the vignettes to make sure things are running smoothly. You'll go where you're needed each night."

When we reached the front door, Justine opened it and waved me through. "Have fun tonight. If you survive, then you can start tomorrow evening at seven o'clock."

The door banged shut in my face, the sound echoing up through the portico.

CHAPTER FIVE

"Well," I said to the door.

I looked to see if Zach was watching, but a shutter had been rolled down over the window. I turned around and looked at the bright day outside the portico's shadow, too stunned for the moment to get my feet moving. That had been the strangest, most unconventional job interview I'd ever had, and what had Justine meant by saying I could start tomorrow "if I survived"?

"She was just joking," I told myself. "A little haunted house humor, that's all."

I walked back to the motel and just plopped down onto my bed. In my mind, I was still going over the bizarre interview and Zach's weird vibes. I really, really hoped I didn't regret this.

One thing I knew for sure was that I didn't want to go through Nightmare Sanctuary all by myself. There was a reason I had only ever been to two haunted houses. I did not like jump-scares, and I didn't like being in the dark with who-knows-what.

I only knew two people in the entire town, and I seriously doubted Mama would want to go with me. Still, I headed over to the office and found her sitting at the desk behind the front counter. "Hey, Mama," I called.

I swear, she looked relieved when she saw me, like she

had expected me to never return from the interview. "How did it go?" Her voice had just a little too much cheeriness to be convincing.

"They're willing to hire me, but they want me to experience the place first. They gave me two tickets for tonight. Do you think Nick might want to go with me? I don't know anyone in this town outside the two of you."

"Let's find out." Mama had her cell phone up to her ear just a second later, and I could tell from her end of the conversation that Nick wasn't up for the outing. When she hung up, though, Mama smiled at me. "My granddaughter, Lucy, would love to go with you tonight. She's eleven, so she shouldn't get too scared. She's been begging to go to that place for years. Halloween is her favorite holiday."

Oh, great. I was going to have to babysit some creepy horror kid while trying to keep myself from screaming and running away in fear from the job I so badly needed. It was going to be a fantastic night.

I was due to meet Nick and Lucy in the motel office at seven, which left me with a couple of hours to kill. Before I wrapped up my conversation with her, Mama had produced a tray of cinnamon rolls, saying her best friend worked in a bakery and had stopped by with some of the day's leftovers. She insisted I take three of them, and I didn't argue. It would be an unorthodox dinner, but a free one.

I savored two of the cinnamon rolls while I sat on the bed and watched reruns of the original *The Twilight Zone* on a local TV station. It seemed fitting, considering what my life had been like for the past twenty-four hours.

I changed back into my shorts and tank top before heading over to the office just a few minutes before seven. I figured there was no need to look professional now that I had the job offer and would be wandering through a dark

31

haunted house. It wasn't like they were going to be able to see me.

The tow truck was just pulling to a stop in front of the motel, and as I watched, Nick sprang out of the driver's side. I braced myself for the creepy horror kid as I saw the passenger door swing open. I was surprised, then, when Lucy came around the front of the tow truck wearing denim shorts, a pink T-shirt, and matching pink sneakers. Her hair was a giant mass of dark curls that someone had tried—and failed—to tame with a headband. A pink one, of course. Lucy was grinning, and when Nick waved to me, she ran right over.

"Hi, you're Miss Olivia, right? Thank you, thank you, thank you! I've been begging to go to the Sanctuary for years, and you're the first person to say yes!"

Wow, this kid has a lot of energy. "I haven't been to a haunted house in more than twenty years," I told her solemnly. "You might have to hold my hand if I get scared."

Lucy planted her hands on her hips and stuck out her chin. "I promise!"

Nick gave us a ride to the Sanctuary, using a narrow fold-out center seat for Lucy. It was a squeeze, but it sure beat walking. He also promised to wait for us while we went through. I asked him three times if he was certain he didn't want to join us, but every time, he was adamant in his refusal.

The dirt road that led to the Sanctuary was packed with cars, both coming and going. I was sure Saturday had to be their busiest night. Nick wound up parked about as far from the building as possible, but Lucy and I assured him we could hoof it, no problem. I walked, but Lucy bounded, sometimes getting a short distance ahead of me before circling back. She flapped her arms as she zoomed past me. "I'm going to Nightmare Sanctuary!

I'm going to the haunted house!" she said in a singsong voice.

At least one of us was excited.

There was a line for the ticket window, but the wait was short. When it was our turn, I found myself face-to-face with Zach again. He looked just as surly as he had earlier. He turned away as soon as I stepped up to the counter. I was thinking how rude he was when he turned back to me with an envelope in his hands. He thrust it at me wordlessly.

"Um, thanks," I said. My name was on the front of the envelope, and two tickets were inside, so Lucy and I stepped over to the front doors. A tall, excruciatingly thin man in a black top hat and a long black coat peered down at us. "Are you sure this is what you want to do?" he asked in a menacing voice.

Okay, this wasn't really scary. I wanted to tell the guy to get himself to the Lusty Lunch Counter for about a hundred cheeseburgers, but he was just a guy in a costume. I smiled at him. "We're sure."

Even as I spoke, I felt Lucy press up against my side. She slid her hand into mine. When I looked down in surprise, she gazed up at me with wide eyes. "I'm, um, just making sure you don't get scared," she said, her voice barely above a whisper.

I gave her fingers a squeeze. "Thanks."

We stepped into the entryway, and it looked so different from the sunny, welcoming space I had been in just a few hours earlier. Stanchions had been set up to form the line, and people snaked back and forth across the entire expanse of the room. It wasn't just the crowd that made it feel so different, though. Low lighting emanated from purple bulbs in the chandelier high above us, and some kind of recessed strobe light flashed intermittently, making it seem like a thunderstorm was raging outside the windows. The same kind of spooky orchestral music I had heard while on hold with Justine was playing quietly from hidden speakers.

Lucy and I joined the line, and I was actually grateful for the wait. The boredom forced Lucy to relax a little, and the time let me absorb every detail of the room, which had incredible crown molding and a massive fireplace with an ornately carved mantel. They definitely did not build hospitals like this anymore.

When we finally reached the front of the line, we were ushered into a narrow space below the staircase by a young woman with acid-green hair. We had been lumped in with what appeared to be two couples, and I hoped they didn't mind us tagging along on what was probably a date night.

Lucy's trepidation had returned in full force, if the strength of her grip on my hand was any indication. We followed the two couples down a dark hallway lit only by wall sconces with dim bulbs. It was dark, sure, but not too dark, and I wondered why I had felt so terrified all those years ago when I had gone through the two haunted houses.

We turned a corner and found ourselves in a scene that looked like an old cemetery. Even the half-dead grass covering the ground looked real, and behind tilting head-stones rose a facade that looked like a mausoleum. It was an impressive set.

A woman dressed in a dirty white nightgown popped up from behind one of the headstones right as the first couple in our group walked past, and I heard a scream, followed by nervous laughter. As we continued, another woman appeared from behind a tall monument. She, too, was wearing white, but her dress was clean and practically glowed in the darkness. It seemed to dance around her ankles. She had sunken cheeks and dark eyes, and her long black hair streamed out behind her, despite the fact there was no wind in the room.

The woman walked gracefully across the grass. As she got closer to us, she opened her mouth and began to wail. It was low at first, but it quickly grew in pitch and volume. The sound became so uncomfortably loud that I finally had to wrench my fingers out of Lucy's grip so I could clamp my hands over my ears. I looked down and saw that Lucy was covering her ears, too.

The two couples began to hustle to the door on the other side of the scene, which was made to look like the entrance to another mausoleum, and Lucy and I were right on their heels.

I finally dropped my hands as we entered another short hallway. Electric candles flickered from their perches on low outcroppings on the walls, and I realized the mausoleum theme had continued into this space. The walls were made to look like bodies had been interred inside them, and fake stone markers had names, dates, and even epitaphs on them.

I was so busy reading the markers that I was surprised when Lucy suddenly yelped. I looked at her and saw that she was staring behind us. She darted in front of me, using me as a barrier between herself and whatever lurked behind. I turned slowly and saw blood-orange eyes staring at me. I jumped in surprise, almost knocking Lucy over in the process.

The eyes belonged to one of the most beautiful women I had ever seen. She had flawless dark skin and black hair that was pulled up in a high coiffure. Even in the dim light, I could see her sharp cheekbones and full lips.

Those lips parted to reveal gleaming fangs. *Ah ha, a vampire lurking in the mausoleum!* I mentally applauded Nightmare Sanctuary for a good show so far.

The vampire leaned closer to me, and her wide eyes filled up all of my vision. When she spoke, her voice was rich and confident. "Welcome to the family, Olivia. You're going to love it here with us." She winked at me, then stepped back into the shadows so quickly it seemed like she had disappeared.

I leaned forward at the waist, peering into the darkness, but I couldn't see her at all. How had she known my name? Even if the employees here knew there was someone new named Olivia joining the team, she couldn't have possibly known that person was me.

Lucy tugged on the hem of my shorts. "They're getting ahead of us."

I turned and saw she was right. The couples had already disappeared through the doorway at the end of the hall. Quickly, Lucy and I followed, catching up to them as we entered a scene that included an entire—albeit down-sized—pirate ship.

Our path through the scene went up onto a low catwalk that spanned what looked like actual water. Fog drifted across it, and vines hung down from tree branches above. I really felt like I was looking for pirates on a trop-ical island as I batted a vine out of my face.

There was a crate about the size of a small SUV next to the pirate ship. One side of it had a glass window, and through it I could see a mermaid swimming in water. She gave her silver tail a flick and swam upward, and her head appeared above the edge of the crate. She rested her arms on the wood and smiled down at us. She had a wide, friendly face, but her smile looked slightly wicked. Maybe it was the green cast to her skin that made me think that. I squinted. Was her skin actually painted green, or was it just the lighting in the scene?

The mermaid brought a hand up to push her long, thick golden hair out of her face. "She's heeere!" she sang in a high voice. She started to laugh, and everything went black.

CHAPTER SIX

I screamed even louder than Lucy. Did I mention that I don't like the dark? I hadn't been scared before, but the vampire knowing my name had thrown me off. It somehow made me feel vulnerable. Being singled out by the mermaid only increased my feeling of discomfort.

The lights snapped back on, and I screamed again. There was a pirate with rotting skin standing in front of me, the edge of his tricorn hat bumping against my forehead. "Welcome aboard, Olivia!" he boomed.

That was it. I snapped. I pointed down at Lucy, who was somewhere behind me, emitting high-pitched little shrieks. "She's just a kid!" I yelled. "How dare you terrify a child like that?"

The zombie pirate threw back his head and laughed heartily. When he looked at me again, he winked. "Exactly who am I terrifying, now?"

And then I realized Lucy's shrieks weren't from fear. She was laughing. When I twisted around and looked down at her, she pointed at me. "He scared you so bad!"

I looked up at the mermaid, who was laughing, too. I turned back to the pirate. He was almost exactly my height, but he seemed larger as he stood there with his arms crossed over his ratty red velvet coat. "I'm sorry," I stammered. "Sorry. I thought she was upset."

Over the pirate's shoulder, I could see the next group entering the scene. I turned and walked as quickly as I could, herding Lucy in front of me. She was still giggling as we went into the next scene, which looked like an abandoned hospital. I was breathing heavily, feeling embarrassed and flustered. I had just yelled at a soon-to-be coworker, and I felt miserable about it.

Then again, I told myself, maybe the pirate deserved it for scaring the pants off me. What was this? Some kind of hazing for new employees?

I squeezed my eyes shut and pinched the ridge of my nose. Of course. After I picked up our tickets, Zach must have sent word around so everyone knew what I looked like, what I was wearing, and which group I was in. When Justine had told me the job would be mine if I survived the evening, she probably knew what was in store for me. The question was, why bother to do this? Did Justine simply want to ensure that I wouldn't get scared if I wound up working in the dark, like she had said I might? Or was there more to it?

I opened my eyes just in time to avoid tripping over a silver gurney covered in what looked like bloody rags. Thankfully, I made it through the hospital scene without anyone calling me by name or nearly giving me a heart attack. I took a few deep breaths, tried again to concentrate on the excellent craftsmanship of the sets, and forced my shoulders down from their spot up by my ears.

Lucy, at least, had completely gotten over her initial fear. She was several feet ahead of me, and as she turned her head from side to side to take it all in, I could see how wide her grin was. The two couples we had been with had left us in their dust, so it was just the two of us, but Lucy didn't seem to mind taking the lead into the unknown.

The next scene we walked into was truly breathtaking. It looked like we had stepped outside and into an actual forest. Bare trees with thick trunks and a riot of branches filled the space. The ground beneath our feet was grassy, and above us, the lighting was done in such a way that there seemed to be a full moon peeking between the branches of the trees.

We emerged into a sort of clearing, where three figures were bent over a huge black cauldron. The fire beneath the cauldron looked real, and I could see what looked like actual smoke rising from it, curling around the sides of the cauldron before drifting into the darkness above. If it wasn't real fire, then it was an incredible effect.

As we got closer, I realized the figures were two women and a girl. The girl looked to be about Lucy's age. She was wearing a black knee-length dress with white tights and black boots that had pointed toes. The younger woman looked like she might be in her late twenties or early thirties, and her long blonde curls cascaded over a red velvet cloak. The other woman was much older, her back rounded underneath her black shawl and her form much too thin for her voluminous floor-length black dress. Her gray hair was pulled back into a bun, but so many wispy strands were sticking up around her head that she looked like she had a sort of halo.

The blonde one walked right up to me, and I braced myself for hearing my own name on a stranger's lips yet again. Instead, she said, "You're not me. Not anymore."

Before I could respond, the old woman stepped up next to her. "But you aren't me. Not yet."

"Who are you, then?" continued the blonde. "Who is Olivia Kendrick, really?"

"*What* are you?" asked the old woman.

That was an odd question. Somehow, this third encounter with strangers who knew my name seemed creepier than the others. I felt like the two women weren't so much looking at me as they were looking into me, and I instinctively took a step back. I wasn't going to yell at anyone again, but I wasn't going to stick around, either.

I looked toward Lucy, only to realize she wasn't there. I felt a brief stab of panic, but then I spotted her a short distance away. She was holding hands with the girl, and the two of them were walking into the cluster of trees at the back of the scene. That sight spooked me even more, and I called her name sharply.

It was only after shouting her name three times that Lucy finally turned, and I waved her over to me. The witch girl said something to her, then dropped her hand.

Once Lucy was by my side again, I put a firm hand on her back and steered her out of there. I didn't even look up at the two women again, though I knew they were still staring at me intently. I could feel it.

The rest of Nightmare Sanctuary went past in a blur. I was tempted to break into a run just to get out of there, but I didn't want to freak Lucy out. I kept our pace brisk yet slow enough that Lucy was still able to enjoy every bit of it. In fact, once we finally popped out the exit door and I felt the fresh air on my face, Lucy started jumping up and down. "That was the most amazing thing ever, Olivia! You're the best!"

She seemed completely oblivious to my... I wasn't even sure what to call it. Fear? No, it wasn't that severe. I felt more creeped out than anything else. Nightmare Sanctuary was uncanny, and I was about to start working there. Because, no matter how strange the evening had been, I wasn't going to run away from a job that was advertised as being part-time work with full-time pay.

Before we even got into the tow truck, Lucy started relaying every detail of our night to her dad. The windows were down, and when we were still a good thirty feet away, she waved her arms and yelled, "Dad! Guess what? I met a witch! And a gross-looking pirate made Olivia scream!"

The dramatic retelling continued the entire drive back to Cowboy's Corral Motor Lodge, and by then, even I was smiling and adding in a few details. Now that we were back in the real world of neon signs and paved roads, it was easier to brush off my strange introduction to my co-workers.

Of course, once I was in my room, by myself, I went right back to mulling over what it had all been about. Lucy had given me a big hug before she and Nick headed home, and I was grateful she, at least, had enjoyed her evening so thoroughly.

I woke up on Sunday morning with tense shoulder muscles. In my old life, I would have called and booked myself a massage. Instead, I reached back and did my best to work out some of the knots with my own fingers. Eventually, I gave in and turned my attention to my one remaining cinnamon roll.

By the time I showered, dressed, and walked to the office for a cup of coffee, it was already ten o'clock. Mama was busy checking out some guests, so I just called a good morning to her and sauntered outside. I parked myself on a bench next to the front door. The yellow awning that stretched across the front of the office building gave me plenty of shade, so I could watch the world go by without worrying I was going to sweat to death.

There was a steady stream of cars on the street, so I figured the actors portraying the cowboys Tanner and McCrory were going to have a big audience for their shootout later.

I wasn't used to having nothing to do. In Nashville, I'd always had something to do. Working in marketing meant there were some things that had to be tackled after hours or even on the weekends, and if I wasn't working, then there had always been errands to run or tasks to do around the house. Here in Nightmare, I was staring nine hours of nothing right in the face, and I didn't like it.

To be honest, I had been too busy in Nashville. I never liked saying no to things, and although some of those things were a lot of fun—like Sunday brunch with my girl-friends—it was still too much. Maybe, I had told myself time and again, if I hadn't been so busy, I would have noticed Mark squandering away our money.

So, basically, I had to find a balance between completely overwhelmed and bored out of my skull. Maybe I could strap a six-shooter to my hip and pretend to run bad guys out of town.

In the end, I settled for watching more reruns on the TV in my room. I also went back to the Lusty Lunch Counter for a late lunch. This time, though, there was no free entertainment.

I was actually looking forward to heading to Nightmare Sanctuary for work that evening. I was that bored. I real-ized I had never been told what to wear, but based on what I had seen the night before, casual was the way to go. Zach had upgraded to a clean Nightmare Sanctuary T-shirt before working the ticket booth, so I figured I would get an official shirt, too, or they would put me in a costume. In the meantime, I chose a pair of black jeans and a plum-colored knit top.

Soon after, I was on my way to my new job. The sun had just dipped behind a distant mountain as I crested the hill, and when Nightmare Sanctuary came into view, it looked more creepy than it had the previous two times I had seen it. In the daytime, the bright sun lessened the effect of the place. At night, the former hospital was simply harder to see, which made it less imposing. Twilight was the real sweet spot for spooky.

I was steeling myself for more bizarre experiences as I walked toward the building. When I got closer to the sign, I could see there was an addition to the jumble of old mining equipment beneath it. Someone had draped a body across one of the giant gears. The head lolled backward over the edge of a cog, and the legs were splayed. The prop was dressed in tight faded jeans and a plaid Western shirt, which had rips across the chest that were rimmed in blood.

"Wow," I said under my breath as I stepped closer. The body looked so realistic.

The tall, thin man who had ushered us inside the night before was walking toward me from the direction of the front doors, and he stopped when he reached the rusty old gear. I was just about to tell him what an amazing job he had done when he clapped both hands over his mouth and stared wide eyed at the body. He slid his hands downward and clasped them together as a cry of shock escaped his lips.

Was this guy pretending the body was real in an attempt to scare me? This had to be more of the hazing I had gone through the night before. Determined to prove I wasn't falling for it, I walked right up to the body and gazed down at its face. The unfocused eyes stared skyward.

I bent forward for a closer look. I recognized that face.

It was the man from the diner. The one who had been arguing with the man in the suit.

This wasn't a prop I was looking at. There was a dead man at my new job.

CHAPTER SEVEN

I sucked in a gasp and took a step backward. That drew the attention of the thin man, who seemed to notice me for the first time. "What have you done?" he wailed.

I shook my head wildly. "I just got here. I walked up right as you did."

He didn't answer me, but he kept his eyes fixed on me as he produced a walkie-talkie from somewhere underneath his long black coat. I couldn't hear what he said into it, but in what seemed like only a few seconds, I heard the sound of running. There were three people sprinting toward us, including Justine. She began to fire off orders. "Malcolm, call the police. Clara, tell everyone to gather in the dining room for a briefing. Olivia"—I jumped at hearing my name included on the list—"go get Zach. I want him to put a team together to block the road at the gallows. Take coupons and tell them to come back tomorrow. No one gets through except emergency vehicles, and no one says anything about this to outsiders."

Malcolm—the tall, gaunt one—was already holding a cell phone to his ear, which looked so incongruous with his top hat and coat. The one Justine had called Clara was already sprinting back to the building. As for me, I was simply frozen for the moment, too shocked to do anything but nod my head dumbly.

"Oh, no," Justine said with a moan. She had stepped closer to the body. "It's Jared Barker. Why is he dead on our front step?"

The name rang a bell for some reason, and it was that awareness that finally got my feet moving. As I sped toward the ticket window, I asked myself why it sounded familiar. I didn't recall hearing the man in the suit call Jared by name during their argument at the diner. I realized it was the last name that had pinged something in my memory, and I thought back to my walk down High Noon Boulevard. The guy who had shoved a flyer for a UFO watch party into my face had said it would be held at a place called Barker Ranch. It was a common surname, sure, but in a town as small as Nightmare? The dead man and the ranch had to be related somehow.

Zach wasn't at the ticket window when I got there, so I went inside and ran down the hallway that I knew led to Justine's office. There was no sign of anyone. Justine had sent Clara to gather the staff in the dining room, so I decided to look there. Of course, I had no idea where that might be.

Fortunately, when I returned to the entryway, the woman who had been wailing so loudly in the cemetery scene the night before was gliding across the stone floor.

"Excuse me!" I called. "Can you tell me how to get to the dining room?"

The woman looked at me with her dark eyes, then gestured for me to follow her. Her voice was low and husky. "Come. I will lead you."

Lucy and I had been in the western side of the building the night before, entering the haunt to the left of the front doors. The woman I was following now went into the eastern wing, entering through a wide wooden door not far from where I had just been.

We went down a hallway dotted with doors, and I saw

45

other people hurrying ahead of us. Everyone was turning left about halfway down the hall, and when I did the same, I found myself in a huge room with windows that looked out over the wilderness behind the building. It was, clearly, the dining room: heavy oak tables were lined up neatly across the room, with matching benches for seating.

I scanned the faces in the room, hoping to see Zach, but I had no luck. Instead, I saw Clara and dashed over to her. She turned to me with wide lilac eyes. Her face was thin and pointed, and she had pinned daisies into her blonde hair. "You're the new one. Olivia." Her voice had a childish sound to it.

"Justine told me to find Zach, but he wasn't at the ticket window. Do you know where he might be?"

Clara's eyebrows knit together. "You're right. I didn't see him as I passed." She glanced at her watch. "Theo can do it. He should be getting up about now."

"Great. Um, who's Theo?"

"He's about your height. Shoulder-length brown hair, brown eyes…" Clara began looking around, then shouted, "Theo!"

"Clara, what's going on?" said a voice behind me a moment later. I had already known from Clara's description that Theo was the zombie pirate I had yelled at, but I couldn't figure out how he had snuck up on me. I hadn't heard his approach at all. At least he wasn't in costume yet, and without all the rotting skin, he was actually really good looking. Or he would be, when he wasn't frowning.

"Olivia will fill you in on the way to the gallows. Justine has work that needs to be done." Without waiting for a response, Clara sidestepped us and headed toward what I recognized as the three witches.

I quickly told Theo that there was a dead man out front, and that we had been instructed to keep visitors at bay. I'm not entirely sure how coherent I sounded as I spoke, but Theo, at least, understood. The second I was finished talking, he turned slightly and shouted, "Amos! Vivian!"

A woman in blue jeans and a polka-dotted blouse was just walking into the dining room, and she looked up, then sped toward us. She was petite, and between her outfit, her red lipstick, and the red bandanna holding her dark hair back from her face, she looked distinctly vintage. A man appeared at her side a few seconds later. While Vivian looked like Rosie the Riveter's cousin, Amos looked like he should have been working in the mine: he was broad and muscular, and he gave off an intimidating feeling, even though his expression was worried as he gently took Vivian's hand.

"This is Olivia. She'll explain while we walk." Theo turned on his heel and strode toward the door, and we all hurried to follow. I hadn't expected to be put on the spot, and I made a few false starts before I finally got all the details out. By then, we were standing in the entryway, where Theo called us to a halt.

He disappeared down the hallway to Justine's office, and when he returned a minute later, he had bundles of what looked like tickets in his hands. He began to hand them around to us, and I saw they were the discount coupons Justine had mentioned. "Let's go," Theo said grimly.

Nightmare Sanctuary didn't open its doors until eight o'clock, but Theo told me to expect early arrivals. Some people would rather wait for the place to open, he explained, than wait in the unpredictable lines later in the evening.

As we walked down the dirt road toward the gallows, we heard sirens in the distance. We all squeezed onto the barely-there shoulder of the road just before two police cars and an ambulance rounded the corner ahead.

Once we reached the crossroads where the gallows were, Theo instructed us to fan out across the dirt road. "Right now, we just need to create a barrier," he told us. "As traffic picks up, we'll direct people to go left and head back into town that way. Tell them we had to close for unexpected maintenance."

I mean, I guess cleaning up a dead body counts as maintenance work.

Theo had been right. We hadn't stood there for more than three minutes before a car pulled up. Vivian swept over to the driver's side, passing a few coupons through the open window. I couldn't hear her, but I could see the way she was smiling in a friendly-yet-apologetic kind of way. Her expression seemed to say, "What can you do about these things, am I right?"

I knew people working at haunted houses had to be good actors, but Vivian was absolutely slaying. She gave no indication how upset and worried everyone was back at the haunt.

It wasn't long before we had a steady stream of cars approaching us, and we took turns sending people down the road to their left, away from Nightmare Sanctuary. By the time the last of the daylight faded from the sky, there was a backup of cars. It was a shame to think how much money the haunt was missing out on. Sunday nights probably weren't as busy as Fridays and Saturdays, but it was clearly still a popular night for tourists to scare themselves silly.

At some point, Malcolm came out to give each of us a bottle of water and a bag of potato chips. It wasn't much, but it helped. I was covered in a layer of dust from the road and tired of apologizing to people over and over again. Earlier in the night, people had been disappointed, and a few were actually angry. By the time we got our snack, people seemed eager to pop their head out of their car window and ask, "So what's going on? I heard the police are there!" We could talk about unexpected maintenance all we wanted, but the truth was going to get out sooner rather than later.

The whole evening felt slightly surreal. I hadn't even signed any paperwork or filled out any tax documents, as one normally would on the first day of a job. Instead, I had walked up to a dead body before standing at a dusty crossroads next to Nightmare's old gallows. The waxing moon that rose above the horizon was the perfect finishing touch.

My co-workers didn't talk to me a lot, but I didn't take it personally. They weren't talking to each other a lot, either. I assumed it was because they were each in a mild state of shock at first. As we got more and more busy, though, it was simply because we were all hustling to keep up with the traffic.

I looked at my watch after I finished off the last of my water. It was ten o'clock, and I had no idea how much longer we would need to stay out there. I dropped my head and rolled it around, giving my neck a bit of a stretch.

I heard the slam of a car door behind me and turned to see one of the police cars. No one would buy the maintenance excuse now. I was surprised when the officer who was walking toward us called, "I'm looking for Olivia Kendrick."

No lie, my first instinct was to turn and run. I felt guilty, even though I hadn't done anything wrong. Instead, though, I raised my hand tentatively, like a kid in school. "That's me."

The officer waved me over to the back of his car, and he pulled a notepad out of his pocket as he leaned against the trunk. "I'm Officer Reyes. I understand you were one of the two people who discovered the victim?"

"The victim?" I blurted. "What, was he murdered?"

49

Even as I said it, I knew Jared Barker hadn't just tripped and fallen onto that machinery cog, nor had he accidentally gotten his chest ripped to shreds. Of course he was a murder victim. My brain had simply been avoiding the concept all night. I guess it was some kind of emotional self-preservation.

Officer Reyes looked at me like he wanted to retort, but instead, he proceeded to ask me questions. I walked him through my arrival at Nightmare Sanctuary, then added what I had witnessed in the Lusty Lunch Counter between Jared and the man in the suit.

"Emmett Kline," Officer Reyes mumbled. He asked me a few more questions, then thanked me and told me I could return to my job.

It wasn't until midnight that Theo told all of us to head back to the haunt. By then, we hadn't needed to turn away a single car for twenty minutes. Theo explained that Nightmare Sanctuary only stayed open until midnight, so it was safe to call it quits. "But," he added, "we're wanted in the dining room for a meeting."

When I walked into the dining room, my sneakers leaving little dust specks in their wake, I realized that when Theo had said "we," he had meant the entire staff. Shortly after we had joined those already sitting at the tables, Justine walked onto a small platform at one end of the room.

"Someone murdered Jared Barker and left him on our doorstep," Justine began. She gazed around at all of us darkly. "Either it was one of us who killed him, or it was someone trying to make it look like one of us."

"How did he die?" someone near the front asked.

"His neck was broken. Plus, there are claw marks all over his body, like an animal attacked him," Justine said bluntly.

"Oh!" I said softly, more to myself than to the people around me. "He was killed by an animal!"

Justine somehow heard me despite being at the opposite end of the room. "No. These marks were intentional. Thoughtful. Animals aren't the only creatures with claws, Olivia."

CHAPTER EIGHT

I walked home that night while looking behind me more than in front. If there was some kind of clawed murderer on the loose in Nightmare, then I at least wanted to see them creeping up behind me before they killed me.

The next morning, the sound of loud knocking brought me out of a dream about walking down an endless line of people, telling each one of them, "I'm sorry, we're closed due to murder."

I tugged at the hem of my sleep shirt, just to make sure all the important body parts were properly covered, as I stumbled to the door. I opened the door with one hand while stifling a yawn with the other.

Mama was standing there, and she thrust a cup of coffee toward me. I gratefully accepted it, then waved her in. I had been so exhausted after I got back from the Sanctuary the night before that I had just thrown my clothes into a heap on the table. I hastily swept them onto my bed and told Mama to have a seat.

"Thanks. I can't stay long," she said as she settled in. "Benny is in Phoenix right now with a sick uncle, so I'm on my own. At least Mondays are slow as molasses once the last of the weekenders check out."

I looked at my watch and saw it was almost eleven

already. I knew I had been exhausted, but I was still surprised to have slept so late.

"Anyway," Mama continued, "I heard what happened out there. You okay?"

I nodded. "I'm fine, just spooked. Did you know Jared Barker?"

"Of course. His family has been in Nightmare for about as long as mine." Mama clucked her tongue. "Such a shame. That place out there…" She mumbled something unintelligible, though I thought I caught the word "unnatural" in the middle of it.

"It is a shame," I agreed. "I'm sorry for all of Jared's family and friends."

Mama fixed her gaze on a point somewhere behind me. "Did you see him? His body?" she asked. I knew she was trying to make it sound casual, but she couldn't hide her curiosity.

I gave her the simple version of what I had seen, saying it had looked like an animal attack.

"Hmm," was all Mama answered. She pressed her palms against the table and pushed herself up. "Well, now that I know you're okay, I'm heading back to the office."

"Thank you for checking on me. And thank you for the coffee." I walked Mama out, then turned around, leaned against the door, and realized I was starving.

I had showered before bed the night before, since there was no way I wanted to get all that dust under the sheets, but I took another shower just to help wake me up. I fished a blue silk sundress out of my suitcase. It was a little fancy for wandering around Nightmare, but it would help keep me cool. Like my purse, it was one of the items I had refused to sell, no matter how desperate I was for the money.

This time, when I walked into the Lusty Lunch Counter, the server who had been behind the counter on both of my other visits didn't even ask me what I wanted to drink. I had a glass of water in front of me before I had even finished getting comfortable on the stool.

It wasn't until I was sticking the first french fry into my mouth that I realized the woman sitting to my left was staring at me. I let the fry fall to the plate and turned to her. Did I have ketchup all over my face or something? If I did, she didn't tell me. She hastily turned back to her own plate.

A mirror stretched behind the length of the counter, and as I ate, I looked up at it and noticed several people sitting in the booths behind me were staring, too. If I happened to meet their eyes in the mirror, they would turn away, but in a minute or two, I would catch them staring again.

And then I started to hear the whispers. The two men sitting to my right were having a quiet conversation while glancing furtively at me. I caught the words "sanctuary" and "coroner."

I waved my server over. I quirked an eyebrow at her and began to open my mouth, but she interrupted me. "Yeah, they're gossiping about you." She didn't bother to lower her tone, and she threw the two men a judgmental look.

I shook my head. "Why?"

"You show up in Nightmare, and two days later, Jared Barker is dead. Not only that, but he's dead at the place where you just got a job."

"His murder has nothing to do with me." The diner grew quiet the second I said the word "murder."

The server shrugged. "Of course it doesn't. But you're new in town, and so people are going to be suspicious. It's natural." She stuck out her hand. "I'm Ella. This is our third day hanging out together, so I think it's time we're on a first-name basis."

"Olivia," I said, shaking her hand.

Ella gripped my hand and leaned toward me over the counter. "Don't pay attention to the nosy neighbors. I don't know who killed Jared, but I know it wasn't you."

Even in the middle of all the suspicion and scrutiny, I was still able to give Ella a genuine smile. "Thanks."

I felt self-conscious while I ate, but at least the two men sitting next to me left soon after Ella had called them out. I was just fishing cash out of my wallet when someone else sat down next to me. I turned and recognized the UFO hunter I had met on Saturday.

"Such a shame," he said to me in a quavering voice. "An absolute shame. He knew the risks!"

Ella had just walked up, and she put her elbows on the counter and cupped her chin in her hands. "Luke, what in the world are you talking about?"

Luke raised his eyebrows. "Jared, of course. I think the visitors might have killed him. He must have done something to scare them or offend them. They're very sensitive, you know."

"The aliens," Ella said in a flat voice, "got their feelings hurt and murdered Jared Barker?"

Luke shook one finger at Ella. "Don't discount my theory!"

"Sure. In the meantime, I assume you want your usual?"

While Luke was distracted by giving his order, I hastily slid off my stool and grabbed my purse. I waved to Ella and widened my eyes in a *Can you believe this guy?* look as I walked behind Luke toward the front door.

Despite sleeping so late, I still took a nap during the afternoon. I was not used to working until midnight, and if that was going to be my life for the next couple of weeks, then I needed to rest up. Plus, worrying about money and murder was just plain exhausting.

I did okay on my walk to Nightmare Sanctuary that evening, right up until I neared the spot on the dirt road where I knew the old hospital building was about to come into view. I wasn't sure what I would see when I reached the crest of the hill, and I had to give myself a pep talk. "Come on, Olivia. It can't be worse than a dead body, so what are you afraid of?"

As it turned out, I didn't have a single thing to worry about. There was no sign that a murder victim had been sprawled on the lawn decor just the night before. Everything looked totally normal. Well, normal for a creepy old hospital, at least.

I was walking through the front doors when I realized I didn't even know where to go to report for duty. Did I have to clock in somewhere? I certainly hadn't the night before, and I hoped fervently I would still get paid for those long hours of turning away customers.

Justine was just walking from the direction of her office when I entered, so I asked her, adding that I still hadn't signed any official employment documents, either. She waved a hand casually. "We'll deal with those soon. They're on the desk, somewhere. In the meantime, I do have a T-shirt for you." She reached into a tote bag dangling from her arm and produced a black Nightmare Sanctuary T-shirt, which she handed to me. "Head down the hall toward the dining room. There's a bathroom on the right with lockers where you can change and store your purse. Come on into the dining room when you're done. It's where we meet each evening to go over job assignments, updates, and that sort of thing."

"A staff meeting," I supplied.

"Exactly, though I don't think of these folks as staff so much as family." Justine gave me a wide smile. "It's a family meeting! Come on."

I got changed and stashed both my purse and the shirt

I had been wearing inside one of the lockers, then walked to the dining room. I noticed as soon as I entered that the mood was a lot less somber this time around. The people already in there weren't what I would call happy, but they didn't seem to be grieving Jared's murder, either. I perched on a bench three rows back from the podium.

I was alone on the bench, and I craned my head around to take a look at the others in the room. The wailing woman from the cemetery scene was pushing what looked like a big washtub on wheels, and the mermaid was in it, her back against one side and her tail sticking out the other.

When I turned my attention to the front again, there was somebody sitting right next to me. I was so startled that I jumped, and I heard a long laugh.

Even without turning to see his face, I knew it was Theo. I recognized that laugh. How did the guy keep sneaking up on me? He already had his zombie makeup on, and he had set his big pirate hat down on the table.

"Hi, Olivia," he said amiably. "You did a great job last night. Where will you be posted tonight?"

"No idea."

Theo reached up and plucked at the sleeve of my T-shirt. "At least you've got your uniform now."

The beautiful vampire who had talked to me during my walk-through with Lucy sat down across from me. I had felt like a total klutz getting my legs over the bench, but she did it in one smooth motion, despite her long, lacy dress. "And don't forget," she said, "it's important to look spooky but helpful."

"Helpful I can do," I assured her. "I'm not so sure about the spooky part."

"You'll do fine, my dear. It wasn't just chance that brought you to us, and I know you're going to thrive here at the Sanctuary. I'm Countess Moreau, though you can call me Mori, like everyone else. It's not just a nickname, you know. It's also the Latin word for 'death.'" Countess Moreau smiled proudly, her fangs gleaming in the glare of the fluorescent lights overhead.

Before I could respond, something brushed against my legs. I jerked back in surprise and looked under the table. A small, wiry gray form darted away from me, running underneath our table with a bent back. It disappeared from view before I could get a clear look.

"What was that?" I asked.

"Oh." Mori sounded uncomfortable. "That was my dog."

I just nodded in response. It hadn't looked like any breed I had ever seen.

It had also been walking on its hind legs.

CHAPTER NINE

Justine shouted a loud "good evening" to all of us before I could comment on the so-called dog. Which was good, because I have no idea what I would have said, but I definitely wouldn't have told Mori her little fur baby was cute. I wasn't even sure it had fur. I hadn't gotten a good look, but I had seen enough to determine it was an ugly animal.

"I know we're all still reeling after what happened yesterday," Justine began as silence fell over the dining room. "I also know you all have the same questions as I do: what does this mean for the future of the Sanctuary, and if Jared was killed by someone in the outside world, did they plant the body on our front doorstep for a reason? I don't know the answer to either of those questions, or to any of the other dozens of questions that keep coming up. I'm sorry. Just remember that the Sanctuary has been through worse and survived. We have each other"—everyone around me spoke the next words along with Justine—"and together, we can face the daylight."

There was a scattering of applause. I wasn't sure what the phrase meant, but it seemed to be some kind of company motto.

From there, Justine shifted into business matters, rattling off a few repairs that needed to be made, some lighting changes in various scenes, and other small things that didn't seem at all pertinent to me. When Justine moved on to where everyone would be posted, I perked up. "Olivia," she called, "you'll be at the front doors, taking tickets and ushering people inside and into the line. You'll be asked a lot of the same questions over and over again, so get with Zach before you start, and he can fill you in."

Great. Asking Mr. Surly for on-the-job training was exactly what I wanted to do.

"Oh, and one more thing!" Justine shifted nervously from one foot to the other. "This goes for all of you, actually. If anyone asks about what happened yesterday, tell them you're not at liberty to comment, but they can look at our website for a statement."

The meeting broke up around seven thirty, giving me half an hour before the doors opened for the evening. I wished Theo and Mori a good night, then made a beeline for the ticket window. Unlike the night before, Zach was actually there this time, looking more sour than ever. I hadn't thought that was even possible.

I stood as far from the window as I could without feeling like I was being completely impolite. "Hi, Zach," I called. "I'm on front-door duty tonight, and Justine said you can give me a rundown of what kinds of questions to expect."

Zach curled his fingers around the edge of the countertop and peered at me. "Where's the bathroom? How long will it take to get through this line? Is it actually scary? Will I get touched by any of the performers?"

"And what are the answers to those questions?" I prompted, when it was clear that was all Zach was going to willingly offer me.

"First hall on your left, about twenty-five minutes, only if you're a chicken, no."

One week, Olivia. You only have to work with this guy for one week. Two, tops.

"Thanks," I muttered. That had lasted all of one minute, which left me with plenty of time before we opened up. I figured I should utilize Zach's information to the fullest by finding my own way to the bathroom.

By the time I returned, there were already people queueing at the ticket window. One of the front doors had been propped open when I had visited with Lucy, so I did the same, then took up a post next to it. Soon, I was tearing the perforated ends of the tickets the early birds had just bought and waving them inside to the rows of stanchions.

Not surprisingly, taking tickets and welcoming people to Nightmare Sanctuary was a lot more fun than turning people away. There were plenty of nervous giggles from the people filing past me, and, as predicted, I was asked the same four questions over and over again.

There was a steady stream of people walking up from the parking lot, and the line for tickets never seemed to get shorter. I couldn't imagine Monday nights were usually that busy, and I had to wonder if all the visitors were because of the coupons we had given out or because everyone wanted to be at the site of the town scandal. Thankfully, only a few people asked about Jared's murder, so I didn't have too much awkwardness.

Malcolm sidled up to me about two hours after we had opened. "I'm relieving Zach so he can have his break. Someone will be here to relive you shortly, too." Sure enough, a minute later, Malcolm's narrow face and tall top hat were floating in the ticket window.

About ten minutes after that, I heard a high voice say, "Hey, Olivia, your turn! You've got the next twenty minutes off." I turned to see Clara, whose lilac eyes were beaming at me. Tonight, her hair was pulled up into a messy bun, and I noticed her ears had the same pointed look as her chin.

I thanked Clara as she stepped into my spot at the front door, then headed to the dining room. My eyes darted around the room as soon as I got in there, and I saw one thing that made me very happy: a table full of snacks and drinks.

I also saw something that made me very wary. Zach had his back pressed against the wall, and Mori was standing directly in front of him. She was shorter than Zach, but her stance gave off an aura of anger and control.

Mori leaned in until her face was just inches from Zach's. "You were working security yesterday, Zach Roth," she spat. "How did you not see anything? Or, maybe you had the best view in the house. Those were claw marks on the man's body."

Zach's eyes widened in what looked like panic, but only for a split second. He sneered and pushed his way past Mori. He hurried toward the door, and I didn't manage to get out of his way fast enough. Zach's shoulder knocked hard against mine as he made his exit, and I spun halfway around from the impact.

"Ow." I rubbed my stinging shoulder while sending the most offended expression I could muster toward Zach's retreating form.

"You okay?" Mori asked.

I turned and saw an angry look on her face, but I knew her emotions weren't directed at me. "Yeah. I don't think he was working security yesterday, anyway."

Mori froze. "What?"

"When Justine came out and saw Jared's body, she started giving instructions to those of us who were standing there. She told me to find Zach, but I never did. I don't think I saw him at all last night, actually."

"Neither did I, but I just figured he was outside, helping turn away visitors."

I shrugged. "Nope. I was out there all night, and he wasn't with us. Frankly, I don't know how all of you put up with him, anyway. Does that guy ever loosen up?"

Mori began walking toward a table. "He has his moments. Grab yourself a snack and sit down." Once I had complied, choosing a package of peanut butter crackers to be my dinner, Mori continued. "Zach fills in as one of the actors a few times a month, but otherwise he works security during the day and handles ticket sales."

"Why do you need security during the day? I would think you'd want it at night."

"We need daytime security to keep us all safe."

I frowned down at the cracker in my hand. "You mean to keep the Sanctuary safe."

"Yes, that, too. Many of us live here at the Sanctuary, you know. There are rooms above us, here in the east wing, plus some other suites scattered around this old place."

My thoughts instantly turned to the room and board possibilities. If I could move in here and not have to pay for a motel every night, I'd have enough money for my car repairs in no time.

No, I told myself. I didn't want to both live and work at Nightmare Sanctuary. I could tolerate the spooky location for an evening, but this was not a place where I wanted to turn out the light and go to sleep. I didn't believe in ghosts, but if I did, this place would have them; I was sure of it.

Something clicked in my brain. "Because this place is open so late, most of you are sleeping the vast majority of the day."

Mori paused for just a beat, then she said, "Exactly." She gestured to the room around us. "This place is hard to resist for teenagers and people who like creepy old places. Even if it wasn't a haunted house, it would still get a steady stream of visitors who like derelict old buildings. Zach keeps kids from breaking in or taking any little souvenirs."

Mori fell silent as I munched away on my crackers. I felt like the sound of my chewing was echoing in the mostly empty dining room. There were a couple of other people in there, apparently on their break as well, but otherwise, the place was empty.

I had just finished my snack and was eyeing a package of cookies when Mori spoke again. She nodded, as if she had just made up her mind about something. "You're part of the family now, Olivia, so I might as well tell you the truth. We aren't really that worried about teenagers coming out here on a dare. Zach started patrolling the grounds after Baxter went missing."

I tilted my head in confusion. "Who's Baxter?"

"The owner of Nightmare Sanctuary. The man most of us owe our lives to."

CHAPTER TEN

Mori sighed and pressed one hand against her heart. The voluminous sleeves of her deep-purple gown added to the dramatic effect, and I thought of a Renaissance painting of a heartbroken maiden. "Most of us here at the Sanctuary never fit in anywhere else. We were... outcasts. Some of us were even run out of town by people who couldn't accept that we were different than them."

I felt a pang of sympathy as I thought of both Mama and the man at the Chamber of Commerce, who had warned me about the "weird people" at Nightmare Sanctuary. Both of them had been so kind to me, so helpful, and it hurt to think they might not be as kind to someone from the Sanctuary, if they ever happened to run into them. Though referring to someone as "weird" and running them out of town were very different things. I wondered what some of the Sanctuary employees might have done that got them rejected by their communities.

"Baxter welcomed everyone," Mori continued. "He was like a father figure to some of us. To others, he was that protective big brother. He didn't care where we came from. He just offered us a home and a job."

"And some of you live here because you don't want to be out in..." I trailed off. The phrase "normal society" had been on the tip of my tongue, but here at the Sanctuary, this *was* normal. The costumes, the fangs, even a mermaid cruising through the hallways in a tank on wheels—it was all normal to the employees of Nightmare Sanctuary.

No wonder Justine referred to them as a family.

I didn't need to finish my sentence. Mori was already nodding. "We feel safer here, yes. We can be ourselves without worrying about what anyone might think."

"What happened to Baxter? You said he went missing?" I remembered Justine mentioning that the haunt's owner wasn't around at the moment, but she certainly hadn't given any indication that he had simply vanished.

"He just disappeared about six months ago. We all woke up one evening, and Baxter wasn't here anymore."

"Would he have skipped town for some reason?"

"No." Even in that one word, I could hear the warning tone in Mori's voice. It was not cool for me to assume Baxter had done something wrong. Clearly, it was generally assumed that someone had done something wrong to him.

Mori sniffed derisively. "There's a local real estate agent who had been nosing around here for weeks before Baxter disappeared. He kept saying he wanted to renovate the place into a five-star destination resort. He has a bit of a shady reputation, and a lot of us think he had something to do with it. Maybe he blackmailed Baxter to force him out of town, or maybe he scared him off somehow. Of course, there's always a third option…"

"You think a real estate agent might kill for a piece of property?"

"Like I said, Emmett has a bit of a dark past, or so the stories go. He's a real piece of work."

I sat up straight. "Emmett? I've heard that name, but where?" I thought back. So much had happened in the past twenty-four hours that it was hard to keep track. I gasped as soon as I remembered. "The police officer who talked to me last night! I told him about seeing Jared at the

Lusty Lunch Counter, where he was arguing with a guy in a suit. The officer mumbled something about an Emmett."

"Three-piece suit, white hair slicked back from a high forehead?"

"That's who I saw arguing with Jared."

Mori leaned toward me, and her eyes locked onto mine. For a moment, I ceased to think about anything but our conversation. Her gaze was almost hypnotic. "Tell me every single word they said to each other," she said in a low voice.

I quickly gave her a blow-by-blow account of the argument, ending with Jared saying, "Over my dead body."

Mori winced at that part and gave a disgusted shake of her head. "That means Emmett is definitely on the police's suspect list. That's good."

"From what I saw earlier, you've got Zach on your suspect list." I realized I had only furthered the case against Zach by talking about his absence in the wake of Jared's murder.

"Zach and Emmett are definitely at the top." Mori still had her eyes on mine. "Don't tell anyone my suspicions."

Again, I could feel something vaguely hypnotic in Mori's gaze. It was almost like a tugging at my mind, trying to steer me in a desired direction. I blinked rapidly a few times to clear my head. "Don't worry, they're on my list, too. I'm the outsider here, and I'm certainly not going to start running my mouth about my own theories, or anyone else's."

Mori's eyebrows drew together, and she sat back. After a few moments, she simply said, "Good."

I glanced at my watch. "I've got to get back to my post. This has been… enlightening. Thanks for being so honest with me, Mori."

Mori gave me a soft smile, the tips of her fangs barely showing. "My pleasure. Like I said, you're part of the family now, too. I don't know what your story is yet, or how you wound up in Nightmare, but I know this place is where you'll find your happy ending."

I just gave Mori a nod. After telling me so much about what was obviously a tight-knit group, I wasn't about to confess that I was just there to get some quick cash.

I walked back to my post slowly, and I was barely aware of tapping Clara on the shoulder and thanking her for the break. I was too busy thinking about everything Mori had told me about Emmett. I really wanted to know what kind of shady past she had been alluding to, but I had a feeling it was a question best saved for when I wasn't on a short break.

Once I was back on front-door duty, I answered questions, tore ticket stubs, and nodded politely at people as they filed past, but internally, my brain was asking over and over again if Emmett had killed Jared over some real estate dispute. Clearly, Emmett had been trying to goad Jared into selling something when I had overheard the two of them that day at the diner. Now, I was certain that something must have been land, maybe even Barker Ranch. Had Emmet killed Jared because he was trying to remove a roadblock to a real estate deal?

Had Emmett made Baxter conveniently disappear for the exact same reason?

I shivered. It was a warm night, but all those thoughts of murder were giving me a chill.

The crowd finally began to wane about an hour and a half before closing. It seemed that tourists and true crime enthusiasts alike wanted to be in bed at a decent hour on a Monday night. I was still taking tickets and answering questions like a robot, going through the motions without really thinking about what I was doing. I couldn't help it: my brain just didn't have the capacity to make small talk with guests and think about murder at the same time.

An hour before closing, one guest did finally snap me back into the present moment. A tall, muscular man wearing an immaculate olive-green suit and mirrored sunglasses sauntered up to me like he owned the place. Who wears sunglasses at eleven o'clock at night? Pretentious people, that's who, at least in my experience. I dutifully reached out my hand to take his ticket, but he started to brush past me without responding.

"Sir," I said in a polite but firm voice, "I need to tear your ticket."

"It's not necessary," he said in an annoyed tone.

"Actually, it is. You need to buy a ticket to get in, and then I need to get the stub for our records."

"I don't need a ticket." The man finally turned to face me fully. He had wavy light-brown hair, and I figured he had spent a long time in front of the mirror making it look so good.

"You do." I pointed toward the ticket window while silently telling myself to keep at least some semblance of a friendly note in my voice. "You can buy it right over there."

"I don't need a ticket," the man repeated, "because I'm not here to walk through a silly haunted house."

That's it. I am so done with this guy. I crossed my arms over my chest and raised an eyebrow. "Then why are you here, *sir*?" I put emphasis on that last word, just so he'd know I wasn't using it to show respect.

I heard a few quick footsteps behind me, and suddenly, Justine was at my elbow. "It's okay, Olivia!" she said breathlessly. To the man in the sunglasses, she said, "This is the woman I told you about. The one who just got a job here."

I threw a confused glance at Justine, and when I looked back at the man, he was taking off his sunglasses. He had the most gorgeous green eyes I had ever seen, and I kicked myself mentally for thinking such a nice thing about such a rude person. He took a step toward me, and I had to crane my neck up to maintain eye contact. I tried to look as defiant as I could.

When the man just continued to stare at me, Justine said in a strained voice, "Olivia, meet Damien. His father owns Nightmare Sanctuary."

"Oh!" I said, startled. "I heard about your father. I'm so sorry he's missing." Jerk or not, I still felt like I ought to offer the guy my sympathy for his situation.

Damien slid his sunglasses back on and shrugged languidly. "He'll turn up eventually. In the meantime, I'm here to run this circus."

CHAPTER ELEVEN

Damien swept past Justine and me without another word, leaving me staring after him, open mouthed. When I turned to Justine, I saw that her expression looked like a combination of anger and fear.

"Is he always that bad?" I asked.

"Yes," Justine said icily. "Thankfully, he rarely comes to Nightmare."

"What's his deal? Isn't he worried about his father?"

"He doesn't seem to be. We called him as soon as we realized Baxter had gone missing, and you would have thought we were calling to sell him a warranty on his car. He acted like it was all just an inconvenience."

Justine left soon after that, saying she was going to make the rounds to forewarn everyone that Damien had arrived. And she actually used the word "forewarn." Clearly, Damien was not a popular guy at the Sanctuary. Of course, with the attitude he had just given me, it was easy to see why.

Shortly before midnight, after the last of the guests had gone past me, and I was getting antsy to go back to the motel and fall into bed, Justine came by again to tell me Damien had called a meeting for the next day at ten o'clock.

I frowned. "In the morning?" When Justine nodded, I said, "But I thought you all slept during the day?"

"We do. Not only that, but Tuesday is the one day a week the Sanctuary is closed. So we have to get up early on our day off to listen to whatever Damien has to say."

When work finally wrapped up for the night, I walked back to the locker room slowly. Around me, others were either leaving their posts to go upstairs or heading to the locker room like me, and I could hear all the conversations about Damien and what his presence could possibly mean. No one sounded excited about his arrival. If anything, I would have said they sounded scared.

I realized when my alarm went off on Tuesday morning that it wasn't just the nocturnal employees who were inconvenienced by this meeting. By the time I had walked back to the motel, wound down, and gone to bed, it had already been nearly two o'clock in the morning. I got up earlier than I needed to because I didn't want to risk being late for the meeting. Damien didn't seem like the kind of guy who would be forgiving when it came to punctuality.

There were a lot of sleepy faces around me when I walked into the Sanctuary's dining room ten minutes before the start of the meeting. I was surprised to see the mermaid was not only still dressed like one, but she was still in her rolling tank, too. Was she some kind of method actor? I could see that once she wriggled her way into that tail, she wouldn't want to take it back off unless she had to, but it didn't make sense that she would be wearing it on her day off.

I looked around for Mori, but she was nowhere to be seen. Instead, I found a spot at the table where Clara and Malcolm were both sitting. They greeted me with grave nods, asked me if I was doing all right, then fell silent. Looking around the room, I could see that very few people were talking. Those who were whispered quietly to their neighbors. I felt like I was at a funeral.

My watch read exactly ten o'clock when Damien stepped up to the podium. He was wearing a tailored charcoal-gray suit with a black button-down shirt underneath. The colors looked good against his light tan, and I was glad to see he had ditched the sunglasses. It made him look slightly less pretentious. I let a wistful sigh escape my lips. It was a shame he didn't have a winning personality to go with his handsome looks.

"Ladies and gentlemen," Damien began. Like my use of the word "sir" to him the night before, he clearly was not speaking out of respect. I could practically feel the disdain rolling off him. "Since my father isn't here to do it himself, I have come to take over the daily operations and financial management of Nightmare Sanctuary."

"Why did it take you six months to finally show up?" someone shouted. I didn't have to look over to know it had been Zach. There was no mistaking that growling voice.

Damien shot Zach a scathing look. "Because I had hoped that you could all manage yourselves. You're adults, aren't you?" Damien's gaze swept the room and froze on the three witches. The youngest one stared back at him, her chin jutting out. "Well, most of you. My accountant has shown me the latest numbers for this place, and it is clear that without my father, none of you are competent enough to keep things afloat."

Justine was two tables in front of me, and her back straightened defiantly. I could see one of her hands, which was resting on the table, curl into a fist.

"I'm not here because I want to be. I'm here because I have no choice. If Nightmare Sanctuary is going to stay in business, then you need someone to lead you. Or, perhaps, you need someone to negotiate the sale of this property. That's one of the decisions I have come here to make. I want to evaluate this place personally before I act."

The room began to buzz as people muttered to each other and even to Damien. Under her breath, I heard Clara say, "That's not right. We're not in bad financial trouble."

"He wants to inherit as much as he can," Malcolm said bitterly. "We're not in dire straits, but we're also not raking in the cash that he wants so badly. It hasn't been the same since Baxter disappeared."

"What a jerk," I mumbled. This place was so much more than a job for the people seated around me, and Damien was threatening to take all of that away from them without even a hint of sympathy. And for what? So he could get more money?

I had kept my voice low, and I knew there was no way I had been heard by the people at the next table, let alone by Damien. And yet, no sooner had those words come out of my mouth than I felt his eyes boring into me. It was the same look he had given me the night before, after he had taken off his sunglasses. It was a searching look, almost curious. I crossed my arms and stared back, my mouth set in a tight line. If this guy wanted to have a staring contest, then I was up for it.

Finally, after what seemed like a full minute, Damien's jaw twitched, and he returned his attention to the room, which was still buzzing with discontent.

Damien cleared his throat, and all of the chatter ceased. It was clear that although he might be disliked by every single person in the room, he was also feared. Because there was no doubt in my mind the silence was coming from fear rather than respect. Damien went on to say that he would be delving further into the Sanctuary's income and evaluating its expenditures. Again, a hum ran through the assembled group, though it was quieter this time.

The meeting only lasted about twenty minutes. I was annoyed that I had walked a mile in the hot sun, and now I had to do it again for such a short meeting. Damien could have just said those things at Wednesday night's family meeting before the haunt opened. So many people had gotten out of bed for so little.

As I rose along with everyone else, I looked for Mori again. Not only was she absent, but so was Theo. No matter. It wasn't like they had missed much.

My route to the door took me right past the three witches. They looked slightly less creepy with daylight streaming through the high windows and the overhead lights blazing down. In fact, the blonde witch was downright gorgeous. Still a bit spooky looking, though.

"The Prodigal Son has come home," said the old one.

"Only to remember that he's the black sheep of the family," the blonde one added.

"You just got here, but you're a part of the family now, too." The little girl reached out and grasped my hand.

The old woman shook her head, wisps of white hair flying around her face. "He won't like that, oh, no."

"He won't like you." The blonde smiled, as if she were paying me a compliment.

"But *we* like you," the little girl said. She smiled up at me. "My name is Maida."

"I'm Madge," said the gorgeous blonde one.

"And I'm Morgan," the old woman finished.

I gave the three of them a polite nod. "I'm Olivia. But then, I think you already knew that."

All three of the witches laughed.

Damien walked past us at that moment, and he turned his head away. I could have sworn he picked up his pace, too.

"Maybe it would have been better if Baxter had made the deal," said Morgan.

"At least then we would know our fate. This uncertainty is bad for working magic," added Madge.

Maida sighed. "Mister Emmett doesn't like us, either. But he doesn't dislike us. He doesn't care, because he sees money instead of people."

My eyebrows shot up as I looked down at Maida. She was surprisingly insightful for such a young girl.

"What do you mean by 'if Baxter had made the deal'?" I asked Morgan.

"If he had agreed to sell the Sanctuary to Emmett Kline," she clarified.

"He always resisted, and for that, we were grateful," added Madge.

"But Mister Emmett isn't as scary as Mister Damien." Maida's voice was barely above a whisper, and she stepped closer to me so that her shoulder was pressed against my hip.

I heard a loud screech and glanced over my shoulder to see the bench at the table behind me skidding violently across the floor. It hit me right in the back of the knees, and I sat down hard on it. I twisted around to see what had caused the bench to move like that and saw something gray streaking down the aisle between the tables. It couldn't have been more than a few feet high, and I instantly recognized it as Mori's pet. There was no way I could call it a dog, because it definitely wasn't. It didn't even have fur— the gray was some kind of leathery skin. I'd heard of hairless cats but not hairless dogs.

And, of course, there was that whole walking on two legs thing.

The creature turned the corner before I could get a good look. It sure could move fast. I stood and pointed in the direction it had run while turning to the witches to ask them what it was, but I stopped with my mouth open. Two cowboys had just walked into the room. Not through the door, but through a solid stone wall.

"How… What?" I was so shocked I forgot to put my arm down.

Madge turned to see what I was gaping at. "That's Tanner and McCrory." She waved at them and flashed a flirtatious-looking smile.

"What, like those guys who do the fake shootout on High Noon Boulevard?" I asked. In fact, they were dressed exactly like the actors I had seen on Saturday, but these two men seemed to glow faintly as they began to swagger toward the mermaid. I blinked a few times and narrowed my eyes to get a better look. It seemed like I could actually see through them.

"Tanner and McCrory are Nightmare's most famous cowboys," Morgan said proudly.

Maida giggled. "Those actors in town make them die, over and over again, every day."

"How did these actors make it look like they just walked through the wall?" I asked. I finally remembered to lower my arm, but my jaw was still hanging a lot lower than normal.

"Oh, Olivia, you're so funny!" Maida said, swinging my arm as she laughed.

"These two aren't actors," said Madge. "They're the real Tanner and McCrory."

"They're ghosts, of course. After all, they did kill each other more than one hundred years ago." Morgan pointed at me and gave me a lopsided smile. "Someday, when you're a ghost, you'll be able to walk through walls, too!"

CHAPTER TWELVE

My mouth moved a few times before I was finally able to get some words out of it. "You're joking, right?" I asked incredulously.

The three witches shook their heads, their movements perfectly in sync.

"Oh. Well, I need to head out. I'll see you all tomorrow night." I extracted my hand from Maida's and made a hasty exit from the dining room. The entire time, I watched Tanner and McCrory. Tanner had pulled his red bandana down from his face, and he seemed to be having an intense discussion with the mermaid. And I could definitely see right through him to where the wailing woman from the cemetery scene and McCrory were having an equally serious conversation. I told myself it was some kind of optical illusion. It had to be.

Still, though, part of my mind was screaming that ghosts were real, and I had just seen two of them strut through a wall into a crowd of people who thought it was totally normal.

Normal. I couldn't even remember what that was like anymore. Nothing in my life had been normal for a long time. First had come the news that Mark had thrown away all our money and wanted a divorce. I had thought selling the house, my car, and most of my belongings had been my rock bottom. With every mile that got me closer to San Diego, I had felt like I was slowly but surely pulling myself up out of the abyss.

And then I had broken down in the strange little town of Nightmare, Arizona. I was stranded, broke, caught up in a murder investigation, working at a place that might be shut down at any minute by the owner's jerk son, and dealing with co-workers who were nice but utterly bizarre.

I can quit, I told myself. *I can walk away from this place, these people, and this murder, and I can find a new job somewhere else.*

My laugh was more of a choked cry. I needed money, and the sooner I got it, the better. I couldn't afford to quit this job. And besides, as unusual as my co-workers were, they were nice to me. Welcoming. When my life in Nashville had fallen apart, a lot of people I had considered dear friends had walked away from me. Without my money or my social status, I wasn't worth their time. Here at the Sanctuary, I had been hazed a bit, sure, but even on that walk-through, Mori had welcomed me and told me I would love it there. She had told me I was a part of the family now. So had Maida, for that matter.

I sighed. Not only could I not afford to quit this job, but I realized I didn't want to quit. I wanted to stay and get to know these people better. And, more than that, I wanted to help them stand up to Damien.

My body suddenly felt exhausted. All the months of struggle plus the stress and desperation I'd felt since arriving in Nightmare were finally catching up with me. There was a gargoyle statue standing next to the door that led from the entryway to the east wing, and I stopped and leaned my forehead against its chest. The gray stone looked like it was covered in a light layer of green moss, and it was surprisingly soft and warm. I shut my eyes and tried to push out all the thoughts running through my mind.

"Are you okay, ma'am?" rumbled a voice.

I shrieked and jumped backward. The statue shifted, one muscular arm reaching out to offer a handshake. "Sorry if I startled you. I'm Gunnar."

"And I'm sorry I leaned on you. I thought you were a prop." I shook Gunnar's hand once I had convinced myself that my heart was not, in fact, going to leap right out of my chest. "I'm Olivia."

"Yes, I know. I'm glad you're here." Gunnar had a wide smile that revealed a row of long, sharp-looking teeth. He stood at least a foot taller than me, and as I took him in, I realized he even had wings. I couldn't imagine how heavy that costume was, and I wondered why he—like the mermaid—had bothered to get dressed up on the one day the Sanctuary was closed.

Maybe he likes being a gargoyle more than being himself.

I smiled back at Gunnar as best I could, told him to have a nice afternoon, and made a quick exit from the building. The walk back to the motel helped calm me. The hot sun seemed to soothe my overwhelmed brain, though by the time I got back to Cowboy's Corral, I was still pondering Gunnar and his gargoyle getup.

A second shower was in order as soon as I got back to my room. This time, it was as cold as I could stand it. I decided I needed a short nap before lunch, so I sprawled on the double bed and stared at the popcorn ceiling until my mind finally let go of the last thoughts that had been running laps around my skull.

When I woke up, I felt better, but I knew what would really help was my daily cheeseburger and fries. I finished getting ready, grabbed my purse, and opened the door, only to find Mama standing there with her hand raised to knock.

"Hi, Mama!" I said warmly, but her worried look sobered me instantly. I waved her inside. "What's wrong?"

Mama sat down at the table and folded her hands in her lap. She had that look that mothers get when they're settling in to give a lecture, and I suddenly felt like a teenager again. My own mom had given me plenty of lectures when I was that age.

"I hear Damien Shackleford is back in town," Mama said in an ominous tone. "Baxter's boy."

I sat down at the other chair and propped my elbows on the table. "Yeah, he showed up last night. How did you know?"

Mama raised one eyebrow. "I hear things. I understand he came back to get the haunted house's finances squared away."

"That's what he says. He's not well liked at the Sanctuary. The staff can tell he doesn't want to be there, and he acts like he's better than everyone else."

"Damien has a lot of pent-up resentment." Mama fell silent for a moment. She shifted her eyes to the side, and I got the impression she was looking not at the wall, but at a memory. "Damien and Baxter never could see eye to eye, but he wasn't a bad kid. Hopefully, he's not a bad man, either. He might be hard to work with, but remember that his daddy is missing, and he never would have willingly come back to this town otherwise. Please try to go easy on him."

I actually laughed. "You want me to go easy on him? Damien has been rude to me since the second we met. I never did anything to him, but he acts like he's got a grudge against me."

Mama shook her head. "I don't think it's against you as an individual, but against anyone working at the Sanctuary. I'm sorry to hear he's acting like that. I had hoped time might soften him a bit."

"What happened to make him like that?"

"I don't know all the details, though there have been

rumors for years that it had something to do with Nightmare Sanctuary. I just know Damien cut ties with his family and left Nightmare to get a fresh start in the world. I actually felt sorry for the kid."

Family. There was that word again. I thought back to what the witches had said earlier, and I wondered if Damien knew how quickly I had been accepted into the Sanctuary family. Was he resentful of me because he hadn't been welcomed the same way? Even if that were the truth, it still gave him no right to be a jerk, to me or to anyone else.

Mama was looking at me expectantly, so I said dutifully, "I'll try to be nicer to Damien than he is to me."

"I appreciate it. Now, you've had a pretty wild few days. You're stranded in a town you don't know, you got a job at a place that's going through some drama, and you found a murdered man. I think you need to let off some steam, which is why we're going to the saloon tonight. My treat."

I quickly agreed, if for no other reason than the chance to see Mama sitting in a bar. She didn't strike me as the type to go out for a drink. Plus, she was right: I needed to unwind a bit.

Mama bustled off shortly after that, telling me to have my cowboy boots on by nine o'clock. I didn't bother to tell her I didn't own—and had never owned—a pair of cowboy boots, despite having lived in Nashville. I figured it was just an expression. By the time I got to the Lusty Lunch Counter for my late-afternoon cheeseburger and fries, I was downright happy. Okay, maybe not happy, but I wasn't unhappy, either. I was looking forward to going out, and I was feeling grateful for the kindness the people of Nightmare had been showing me.

I had a lazy afternoon, and instead of feeling bored and pent up, I simply felt like I was saving my energy for whatever the night had in store. The phone in my room rang three times before I realized the noise was someone calling me. I just wasn't used to the sound of a normal, hard-wired phone anymore. It was Mama calling from the office, telling me to head up there at seven-thirty for dinner. That woman was single-handedly keeping me from going hungry.

I walked into the motel office right on time and inhaled deeply. Barbecue. And from the smell of it, it was good barbecue. Nick and Lucy were in there, and Lucy ran right over to me and wrapped her arms around my waist. "Hi, Olivia! How's your new job at the haunted house?"

"It's good! I've met a lot of the people who scared us when you and I visited, and, as it turns out, they're really nice."

"Yeah, I hope I can play with that girl again. The one in the black dress."

I wasn't sure I was comfortable with that, but I said, "Her name is Maida."

"Maida. Yeah, she was nice."

Mama was eyeing us, and I got the distinct impression she didn't like the idea of her granddaughter making friends with anyone from the Sanctuary, let alone a pint-sized witch. I changed the subject quickly, asking Lucy about what she had done during her summer break. Before long, we were all seated in the lobby, chatting happily while balancing paper plates piled with pulled pork, coleslaw, and baked beans.

Once we finished eating and cleaning up, Mama disappeared into the back office, saying she was going to freshen up. I had expected her to simply touch up her makeup and fluff up her voluminous hair, but instead, she came out wearing a sparkly black top and a tight-fitting pair of crisp blue jeans.

"Ooh, you're wearing your good jeans!" I commented.

"I don't go out often, so when I do, I have to make the most of it. Let's go!" Mama hugged Lucy, gave Nick a wave, and we were off.

The saloon was on High Noon Boulevard. As we walked there, Mama told me it would be a mix of locals and tourists. "But," she added, "on Tuesday nights, there are more of us than there are of them. Nobody who lives in Nightmare goes near the saloon on the weekends."

Nightmare Saloon didn't disappoint. It was about halfway down the street, and inside, dim lighting threw long shadows across the wooden floor and wall paneling. An upright piano sat in one corner, and a man was playing something that was upbeat but distinctly old-timey sounding.

The bar stretched across the entire back wall of the saloon. Mama headed straight for two empty stools, greeting people at the tables we passed as she went. Clearly, Mama was well known and well liked.

I was halfway through a locally brewed beer when Mama elbowed me gently. "See that table full of women over by the piano?" she said in a half whisper. "The one wearing the red blouse is Jared's widow, Laurie Barker."

I looked as surreptitiously as I could. The women were laughing, and three empty beer pitchers sat in the middle of the table. "Why is she at the saloon? Her husband was just killed!"

"That's exactly why she's here. She's getting drunk, of course. Wouldn't you do the same if your husband had just gotten murdered?"

I mumbled something about husbands and took a long sip of my beer. A moment later, I felt a tap on my shoulder. I turned to see Jared's widow staring at me, her body swaying slightly.

"I hear you're the one who found him," she said.

CHAPTER THIRTEEN

Wow, talk about awkward. The woman was staring at me, and the situation only got more uncomfortable the longer I hesitated. Finally, I squeaked out a "yes." That didn't seem like enough, so I added, "My condolences for your loss."

Laurie laughed bitterly. "How am I even supposed to pay for his funeral? His father turned that cattle farm into an empire, but Jared just didn't have the same business sense. I need money more than I need condolences."

I grabbed my beer and raised it toward her. "I hear you. My husband left me high and dry, too. Well, my ex-husband."

"I guess now all that's left for me to do is to sell the ranch to Emmett," Laurie said.

I noticed she didn't actually sound sad about that being her only recourse. "Emmett is that real estate agent, right?" Of course he was, but I was trying to sound casually interested. "Did he want to buy your ranch?"

"Yes. And I told Jared time and again to take the offer, but he was either too proud or too sentimental to go through with it. It was only a matter of time before he ran that ranch into the ground. He couldn't even keep his cows alive."

Mama and I exchanged a glance. "What do you mean?" I asked.

"I mean some of the cows died." Laurie looked at me like I might be slightly stupid. "It was weird, too. One died, then a few weeks later, another one went, then one died the next month. All of them had been healthy beforehand. Jared was convinced it was something supernatural. You know, he even had the audacity to suggest it was aliens who were killing his cows!" Laurie sighed. "I think he was losing his mind as well as his money."

Laurie wandered back to her table soon after that, leaving Mama and me to stare at each other, open-mouthed. Emmett was already a suspect in Jared's murder, as far as I was concerned, but Laurie had just gone on my list, too. She certainly didn't seem to be mourning the loss of her husband as much as the loss of their money.

Mama's thoughts were clearly heading in a different direction than mine as we spun back around on our stools to face the bar again. "Jared thought aliens were killing his cows?" She looked at me with wide eyes.

"Well," I said, shrugging, "he was letting that UFO hunter host watch parties at his ranch. Maybe the aliens thought they got a free dinner out of it."

Mama burst out laughing, then raised her beer glass and clinked it against mine. "Oh, yeah, you're going to fit in just fine here."

We cut ourselves off after just two beers, agreeing that we were both too old to go for three. When we got back to the motel, Nick came out of the office to meet us. "Where's Lucy?" I asked.

"Oh, her mom came and got her shortly after you two left for the saloon. There was no point in her staying up late just to babysit the motel with me." Nick grinned at me. "I forgot to tell you earlier, but your car should be ready by Friday afternoon."

I braced myself as I asked Nick how much the bill would be, but it was actually a little less than I had expected. I did some quick math in my head and realized that with another week of work, I should be able to pay for my car, pay for my motel, and get out of this town. Still, it was time to confess to Nick that, at the moment, I couldn't afford to pay for all the work he was doing on my car. I felt warmth spreading in my cheeks, and I kept my eyes firmly fixed on the calendar hanging on the wall behind Nick as I answered, "This job pays weekly, but I don't actually know what day I'll get paid."

"That's fine," Nick said quickly. "Your car will be waiting when you're ready."

Mama gave me a sly look. "Are you saying you're just sticking around until you get some money? Because I think maybe you're sticking around to see the drama unfold."

"Oh, no. I've had enough drama to last me for a while, thank you very much!"

Mama proceeded to tell Nick about our encounter with Laurie Barker, and he, too, thought the idea of aliens attacking Barker Ranch's cows was funny. I was grateful the conversation had shifted away from my lack of money, and the mention of the cows brought up a new thought: could Emmett have killed the cows to devalue the ranch? If he really wanted the place, maybe he thought he could convince Jared to sell before more cows died and the ranch wasn't worth as much.

I went to bed still thinking about cows, aliens, and conniving real estate agents. Not surprisingly, my dreams were strange.

It was funny Mama had suggested I was sticking around Nightmare to watch the drama, since the next day had none at all. I slept in on Wednesday morning, had my late lunch at the Lusty Lunch Counter, and walked to work that evening, all without any kind of strange occurrences.

My day had been so normal it actually made me a little nervous as I crested the hill on the dirt road and caught sight of the old hospital building. It felt like I was simply in the calm before the storm. The Sanctuary looked less imposing to me now, but I was still worried about the things happening inside its walls.

When I walked into the dining room, the people already there looked relaxed. I made my way to a table near the front, where Mori was just sitting down next to Theo. "Hi, you two," I said. "We missed you at the meeting yesterday."

Theo snorted. "We didn't miss being there."

"At least he's not here tonight," Mori said. She reached out and put a cool hand over mine. "How are you, Olivia? Getting settled in okay?"

I gave her a lopsided smile. "I'm doing better now that I know Damien isn't here tonight. At least, that's who I assume you're referring to." Now I understood why the mood in the room felt so much better.

"He came all the way to Nightmare to save us from ourselves, and he's already absent," Theo said. "But"—he raised a finger—"no one is complaining about that."

A snarky comment about Damien was on the tip of my lips when I remembered Mama's admonition to take it easy on him. So, instead, I said, "Should we be worried that Damien is missing, just like his father?"

"He isn't missing," Mori said. "Just absent. Rumor has it he's having dinner with a few members of the Chamber of Commerce, trying to butter them up."

Justine started the family meeting right then, and I was again assigned to the front door. I was going to be an ace ticket tearer by the end of the week. As the night wore on, it got easier to push thoughts of Damien and his threats about the future of the Sanctuary out of my mind. The crowd wasn't nearly as big as it had been on Saturday and Monday, but there was a steady stream of people. I had fun greeting everyone and, for the first time, I was truly able to relax and simply enjoy the job. It made the night go by quickly.

I went to bed Wednesday night, feeling optimistic. If I could have one normal day in Nightmare, then maybe I could have another.

I fell asleep with that thought, and it was the first thing that went through my head when I woke up on Thursday. I got through lunch without anything strange happening, and I had a pleasant wander through the shops along High Noon Boulevard afterward. I took a nap, I walked to work, and still, I was on track for Totally Normal Day Number Two.

And then I got to the front door of the Sanctuary. It was open, and I saw Justine standing just inside. There was something about the set of her mouth that filled me with dread. I walked up to her and simply said, "What?"

"Damien wants to see you in his office."

Ugh. "And that would be where?"

"My office. He kicked me out. Of course, it's really Baxter's office." Justine's jaw clenched, and I wondered what she was holding back on saying. I expected it was a long list of unpleasant names for Damien.

"Wish me luck," I intoned.

"Maybe the witches can work a spell to make him more tolerable," Justine said thoughtfully. "I'll go chat with them now. Good luck!"

The hallway to the office felt three times as long as it had the first time I had walked down it. I couldn't imagine why Damien wanted to see me, and my dread only got worse the closer I got to the office door.

The door was closed, so I knocked. The *thuds* my fist made against the giant oak door sounded weak and pathetic to my ears. I had been aiming for strong and confident.

The door was so thick I barely heard Damien calling

for me to come in. I steeled myself and opened the door to find Damien sitting behind the desk, his focus on a stack of papers in front of him. He had taken off the jacket of his three-piece gray pinstripe suit, and the sleeves of his periwinkle shirt were rolled up to the elbows.

I sat down and waited, and it wasn't until Damien had scribbled a few notes before he finally put his pen down and turned his attention to me. He gazed at me the same way he had the night we met, like he was trying to divine some kind of information just by staring at me. I squirmed in my seat and turned my head toward the bookcase on a side wall.

"Tell me how you wound up getting this job," Damien said.

Did Damien call me here to conduct some kind of retroactive interview? I told him about seeing the notice on the job board outside the Chamber of Commerce, adding that when I called, Justine had invited me in for an interview that very day.

Damien picked up his pen again and began twirling it between his fingers. "How long have you been in Nightmare?"

"Since Friday."

"Why did you come here?"

Okay, this was seriously starting to sound like an interrogation rather than an interview. "My car broke down just outside of town. I'm stuck here until it's fixed."

"And then what?"

"And then I get back on the road to San Diego." Oh, dear, had that truth really slipped right out? Knowing I hadn't committed to this job long-term wasn't going to make Damien any friendlier to me.

"You live in San Diego?"

Why did Damien even care where I lived? I just couldn't figure out what he was getting at. "No. I lived in

Nashville, but my careless husband—ex-husband—lost all our money. I had to sell almost everything, and now I'm heading to San Diego to live with my brother and sister-in-law until I get back on my feet. But I broke down here, and I needed a job to pay for the car repairs. I went to the job board, and I found the listing for the Sanctuary. That's how I wound up right here, in your office, having this conversation."

It was everything I could do not to sit back, cross my arms, and say, "So there!"

Damien rested his elbows on the desk while peering closely at me again. "Do you always get what you want in life?" he asked.

Now I was the one staring at him, my eyes narrowed. "Did you not just hear my story? I'm a middle-aged, divorced woman with no money and no home. Do *you* think I always get what I want in life?"

"I wonder," Damien said quietly, more to himself than to me. We continued our staring contest for a few moments longer, then he sat back. "You can go."

Damien's voice followed me out the door. "Oh, and Olivia? Now that you got the job you wished for, you should start wishing for it to last. If we don't find out who killed Jared, I don't think this place will be able to stay open."

CHAPTER FOURTEEN

Part of me wanted to turn around and ask Damien what he meant, but I kept walking. I doubted he would give me an answer, anyway. I walked slowly to the locker room and then into the dining room, my mind buzzing with about five hundred questions. I mostly wondered how Jared's murder could possibly lead to the Sanctuary closing. Was it because the murderer might be one of us working there, and Damien didn't want to risk it happening again?

On top of being worried about the future of the Sanctuary and my job, I was also wondering what that whole meeting with Damien had been about. It had not, as I had suspected, been a more formal interview than the one I had gone through with Justine. He hadn't asked me anything about my skills or my work experience. In fact, it had felt like he simply wanted to know who I was and how I had gotten myself there.

It was clear from the quieter voices in the dining room that everyone else was feeling weighed down by Damien's presence, too. I slid onto the bench that was quickly becoming my usual spot, and Theo turned to me, his zombie makeup looking especially realistic this time.

"You'll be a lot busier tonight," he told me. "Thursday is when the visitors who are in Nightmare for a long weekend show up."

I smiled. "I'm ready! My ticket-tearing skills are top notch!"

Theo winked at me. "One of these days, we need to get you inside the haunt. You miss all the screaming when you're stuck at the front door."

"Thanks, but I'm perfectly happy greeting guests in their pre-terrified state."

As I glanced around during the family meeting, I noticed Zach was sitting by himself at a table near the back. He was rubbing the back of his neck, his eyes darting around the room. I caught myself staring at him and hastily turned my attention back to Justine, but she had just wrapped up. Mori squeezed my arm and wished me a good night, and then we were all off to our posts.

Theo had been right: Thursdays were a lot busier than Wednesdays. Malcolm was the one working the ticket window, and every now and then, he would catch my attention to give me a thumbs-up while looking at me questioningly. I appreciated him checking on me, especially since Zach never even acknowledged my presence when he was working the window. Each time, I would grin and give Malcolm my own thumbs-up in response.

The time flew past so quickly I was surprised when a voice said from behind me, "It's time for your break."

I turned to see it was Zach. He was looking down at his hands, which he was twisting together nervously. I thanked him, and as I began the walk to the dining room, I couldn't help but pause and look back at him. Zach was tearing tickets, but he was shifting from one foot to the other, and his shoulders were rounded. If anything, I would say he looked defensive.

Mori was taking her break, too, and after I grabbed a bag of chips and a package of cookies, I sat down across from her and whispered, "What's with Zach tonight? He seems upset."

"Of course he's upset," Mori answered, not bothering to keep her voice low. "He's not just on *my* list of murder suspects. Pretty much everyone here thinks he killed Jared."

"Have the police questioned him?"

"Not yet."

"If Zach had been on guard duty that day, he would have seen whomever left Jared on our doorstep," I mused. "Or he was on guard duty, and he killed Jared himself. Maybe it was self-defense?" And, I wondered, if Zach had killed Jared, then how had he made it look like an animal attack?

"Zach keeps claiming his innocence whenever one of us confronts him, but he won't say why he wasn't there to see it happen."

"Why in the world would Zach have wanted Jared dead in the first place?" I asked.

"Add that to the list of things we don't know."

Even though Zach had already been a suspect in my eyes, knowing pretty much everyone else at the Sanctuary felt the same way made his guilt seem more likely. It was strange walking back to my post, knowing the guy who was giving me the chance to have a break might have murdered someone just four days ago.

As I got closer to the front door, I could see Zach was talking on his cell phone. He had it wedged between his right shoulder and his cheek so he could continue tearing tickets with both hands while he talked.

"No, I can't see you tonight," he said in a low voice. After a moment, he made an exasperated noise and said, "Fine, but don't come here. Behind the saloon. One o'clock."

Zach ended the call and shoved his phone into the back pocket of his jeans. I hung back a moment, just so he wouldn't realize I had been standing there, eavesdropping, before I let him know I had finished my break.

The first part of my night had gone past so quickly, but once I was back at the door, the minutes crawled by as I kept going over all the questions in my head, again and again. For all of the questions, there was one thing I knew for certain: I was going to be behind the saloon at one o'clock. Was it smart to follow Zach? No, of course not. But I needed this job, and if I could find out what he was up to, it might lead to evidence that he had killed Jared. And once Jared's murder had been solved, there was a better chance that Nightmare Sanctuary would remain open, and I would continue to be gainfully employed.

Plus, I had to admit, I wanted to solve Jared's murder not just for myself, but for the sake of everyone at the Sanctuary.

Once we closed for the night, I retrieved my purse from my locker, then walked out as if I were heading back to the motel. Before I reached the main street, though, I veered right onto a dark side road that I figured would get me to the saloon. There were no streetlights, so no one would see me sneaking toward Zach's meeting point. I didn't want anyone to spot me, especially Zach. I didn't think I could claim I was taking a casual midnight stroll if he caught me.

It wasn't one o'clock yet when I arrived, so I found a hiding spot behind a dumpster in the alley that ran behind the saloon and settled in for the wait. The spot wasn't glamorous, but it gave me a great vantage point. As I waited, I started to question my judgment. What I was doing was stupid and dangerous. It was also smelly.

I had just made up my mind to leave when I heard soft footsteps. I peeked around the edge of the dumpster and saw someone wearing a long coat with the hood pulled up. It was way too warm out for a coat, even at that hour, so I knew the person was trying to disguise themselves. They were doing a good job of it, too. The coat was dark, so when the person stepped back against the wall of the saloon, they virtually disappeared into the shadows.

Zach showed up just a few minutes later, looking around furtively. The person in the coat stepped out to meet him, and Zach froze, his hands curled into fists. At first, I thought Zach and the stranger were squaring off to fight, but then I could hear low voices. I couldn't make out what they were saying, though I could see the way both of them began gesturing to each other. Zach shook his head, his hands flying. I was pretty sure they were having an argument about something.

Zach began to turn away, but the person in the coat quickly closed the gap between them and grabbed his arm. Zach wrenched himself out of the person's grip and whipped around. He pushed his face so close to the other person's that his nose disappeared into the hood.

This time, I didn't hear voices but growls.

The person in the coat jumped backward as Zach's spine suddenly contorted into a hunched shape, pushing his face even farther forward. His back seemed to grow, becoming taller and more rounded. The T-shirt Zach was wearing stretched, and the arms coming out of the sleeves thickened and turned a rusty brown.

No, I realized. His arms weren't turning a different color. They were growing reddish-brown fur. Zach's head was changing, too, his jaws elongating into the shape of a snout. He dropped to all fours and kicked his feet, his shoes flying. Where his feet should have been, I saw giant paws. Zach's jeans ripped, and a tail emerged to stretch out behind him.

I covered my mouth with both hands to keep myself from screaming. I didn't believe in supernatural creatures. At least, not until that very moment. Because I knew, without a doubt, that Zach had just turned into a werewolf right in front of me.

The person in the coat turned and ran. Zach lifted his head and howled, his fangs barely showing in the dark alley, and gave chase.

CHAPTER FIFTEEN

Zach's snarls and the sound of footsteps faded, until I was standing alone in a silent alley. I'm not sure how long I stayed in that exact same position, too shocked to move. If it weren't for the shredded jeans and discarded shoes lying in the middle of the alley, I would have thought I had imagined the whole thing.

I had seen enough werewolf movies to know that was what it looked like when a human turned into one. *But werewolves aren't real,* I told myself firmly.

Unfortunately, my brain argued back. "They're real here," I whispered.

I looked up at the sky as I finally pulled my hands away from my face. There was no sign of a moon from my vantage point, but I thought I remembered seeing it on my walk over. It had been big, but nowhere close to full. That meant Zach had broken some kind of werewolf rule, since I knew—again, from plenty of horror movies over the years—that werewolves only transformed during a full moon.

Of course, it was possible Hollywood had gotten it wrong.

There was also the possibility that I was seeing things. Had I snapped? Had all the stress and drama of my life finally become too much for my mind, and I had just careened over the edge by imagining my rude, potentially murderous co-worker to be a werewolf?

Frankly, I wasn't sure which option was better: that Zach really was a werewolf, or that I only thought he was. Either way, I was scared. My fight, flight, or freeze response shifted from freeze to flight. I started to run.

I went exactly two steps before I slammed into something firm but slightly pliable, and I felt two strong arms encircle me. I screamed and instantly tried to wrestle myself out of my attacker's grip, even as I realized I wasn't actually being attacked.

I also realized the arms weren't covered in reddish-brown fur. Instead, they were gray and slightly textured.

"It's okay, Olivia. It's okay." I looked up to see Gunnar looming over me, still in his gargoyle costume.

Gunnar's arms loosened, and I began to back away. "Oh, no," I said, waving my hands as realization washed over me. "No, no, no. It's not a costume, is it? You... You're..."

"No, it's not a costume," Gunnar said softly.

"You're actually a gargoyle?" My voice rose, and I felt like I was on the verge of letting out another scream. "Zach is a werewolf, and you're a gargoyle? What kind of a place is this?"

"Hush!" Gunnar hissed, leaning down close to me. "Do you want him to hear you?"

"Who?"

"Zach, of course!"

"Right." I took a few deep breaths. I was still trying to accept that werewolves existed, and suddenly, a real, honest-to-goodness gargoyle was standing in front of me. I had thought they were nothing more than statues on old churches in Europe. At least, I told myself, Gunnar seemed friendly enough, unlike Zach.

Something clicked in my mind. "You're following Zach, too, aren't you?"

"Yes. I want to know if he killed Jared. Apparently, so do you. Come on. Let's go somewhere safe so we can talk. There's a good late-night place nearby."

I immediately spun around and began walking in the direction of the Lusty Lunch Counter, but Gunnar put a gentle hand on my shoulder. "It's this way," he said, pointing with his other hand back in the direction of the Sanctuary.

He led me a short distance down the alley, then turned and walked up to a small red door at the back of a building that fronted High Noon Boulevard. He knocked softly, and I saw a little window in the door slide open. Gunnar said something under his breath, gestured to me, then spoke again. The window slid shut, and a second later, the door opened. Gunnar waved me inside, keeping a hand on my shoulder as he followed. I felt like I was going into some kind of supernatural speakeasy.

The door was being held by a small woman with a pointed face, and she reminded me a lot of Clara. While Clara's eyes were violet, though, this woman's were rose colored. "You're responsible for her," the woman said to Gunnar.

"She's trustworthy," Gunnar answered smoothly. To me, he said, "Go right, down the stairs."

I did as instructed, going down a metal spiral staircase that led into the basement. Except when I got there, I realized it was a bar, but totally unlike any I had seen before. All the lighting came from candles that were clustered on tables and niches in the walls. Long, draped pieces of fabric in jewel tones hung down from the ceiling, and under my feet, coordinating rugs covered much of the old wooden floorboards. The tables were arranged in alcoves between curtains, with low stools surrounding them.

I glanced back at Gunnar. "I feel underdressed," I said.

"It doesn't matter what you wear," he said. "It matters what you are."

When I looked at him questioningly, he continued, "This place is run by a family of fairies, so they're friendly to other supernatural creatures."

"That's why the woman at the door said you're responsible for me. Because she's letting you bring a non-supernatural person in."

Gunnar shrugged. "You look like a regular human, at any rate."

"I am a regular human," I said under my breath as Gunnar moved past me and led the way to a table near the middle of the bar. His knees were practically under his chin when he sat down on a stool with purple upholstery, and he rested his forearms on them.

A man who looked like he was related to the woman who had let us in walked up to our table. Gunnar had said they were fairies, and I was trying not to stare at the man's pointed ears as he spoke. "Gunnar, good to see you. Ah, this is the new one in town. Olivia, I believe? Welcome to Under the Undertaker's."

"We're below the coffee shop," Gunnar explained to me. "It's housed in the space that used to be the undertaker's."

"It's a beautiful bar," I said honestly.

The man took our drink orders—after my night, I skipped beer and went straight for a gin and tonic—and as soon as he walked away, Gunnar waved his hand toward me. "Go ahead. I know you have questions."

"If Zach is a werewolf, and you're a gargoyle, then does that mean no one at Nightmare Sanctuary is playing a part? The vampires are really vampires, the witches are really witches, and that mermaid is a real mermaid?"

"Siren, actually. She and the banshee are dating. You

know, the woman in the cemetery vignette with the long, dark hair. It's horrible when the two of them get into an argument. The siren sings and the banshee wails, and everyone is miserable."

"What is Justine?" She had seemed so ordinary. So much like me.

"Justine has the power of telekinesis. She can move objects with her mind. Even those who look normal can be extraordinary."

"Is that why she took over when Baxter went missing? Because she looks like any old human?"

"It's one of the reasons. She can deal with people from the community without making anyone uncomfortable or starting any rumors. Mostly, though, we picked Justine because she's a good leader."

I gestured toward Gunnar. "I guess you can't exactly hang out at the saloon."

"Not exactly. Thankfully, I can come here, and nobody looks twice."

Our bartender returned just then, and after thanking him, I took a long gulp of my drink. I put it down and wrapped both hands around the cold glass. "This is a lot to take in, you know," I said.

"We had a bet going on how long it would take you to realize the truth." Gunnar smiled at me, and I noticed for the first time that his teeth were long and sharp. "I lost, unfortunately. I had my money on week two."

"I have another question," I said, raising a finger. "How did Zach transform into a werewolf tonight? It's not a full moon."

"Zach is a werewolf for three days every month: the days during the full moon. But, at other times, being in situations with a lot of stress, fear, or emotion can cause him to change temporarily. He's probably back in his human form already."

"Without his pants!" I laughed at the mental image.

"One of the downsides to his condition," Gunnar agreed. He gestured to himself with a smirk. Clearly, he didn't have the same problem, since he didn't wear clothes at all. "Another downside is that Zach can only work as a character in one of the vignettes those three nights a month. Well, he could do more nights, but he doesn't want to put on a costume and pretend to be something he's not. When he's in human form, he does security, sells tickets, and does whatever other mundane jobs need doing. It's one of the reasons he's in such a foul mood all the time."

"It's still no excuse for being so rude," I said as I brought my glass up to my lips. I took more of a sip than a gulp this time, then added, "I feel bad for whomever he was chasing tonight. I wonder if there's going to be another clawed-up body in the morning. Oh! No wonder everyone suspects Zach of killing Jared! Jared had those awful claws marks on him, which could have been done by a werewolf." Mori's confrontation with Zach was suddenly making a lot more sense.

"Exactly."

"I still don't understand what Zach could have had against a local rancher. It doesn't seem like they would be crossing paths on a regular basis, especially now that I know the Sanctuary's big secret."

"Clearly, there are a lot more details that we're missing. I really wish I knew who that was he met in the alley."

I told Gunnar about the phone conversation I had overheard. While it didn't tell us who Zach had met, it was clear this was a planned meetup that Zach had been reluctant to attend. "Maybe it was a co-conspirator in Jared's murder," I suggested. "Or someone who knows the truth and is blackmailing Zach."

"Or it could have had nothing at all to do with Jared's murder," Gunnar pointed out.

I sighed. "Maybe we should just talk to Zach. We could clear up a lot of this with one conversation."

"We've tried, and he won't give up anything."

"Has anyone tried speaking to him calmly, or have you all been pinning him against the wall while threatening him?" I asked, thinking of Mori's accusations.

"Well..." Gunnar took a swig of his beer and looked appropriately guilty.

Now I know what a gargoyle looks like when he's embarrassed.

I stared at the ice cubes floating in my glass. "Jared's widow mentioned some of their cows had died strangely. Apparently, Jared thought it might have been an alien attack. I wonder if it could have been a werewolf attack?"

Gunnar shook his head. "I don't know anything about dead cows, but it sounds like something we should learn more about."

"If Zach won't give up any details, then maybe Jared's widow will. I'm going to find a way to have a friendly little chat with her."

CHAPTER SIXTEEN

I woke up Friday morning feeling like I was on a mission. It was time to get some answers so we could catch Jared's killer, keep Nightmare Sanctuary open, save my job, and pay off my debts to Mama and Nick. In my mind, solving this murder was my ticket to San Diego.

Unfortunately, I couldn't just hop in my car and drive to Barker Ranch to talk to Jared's widow, Laurie, since Nick had said the repairs wouldn't be finished until later that afternoon. Besides, even if my car was ready, I still didn't have the money I owed Nick for it.

I mentioned my transportation dilemma to Mama while I was drinking my morning cup of burned coffee in the lobby. I didn't want to tell her that one of my co-workers was suspect number one in Jared's death, but I did tell her that I was interested in finding the truth so the Sanctuary's reputation wouldn't be tarnished.

Mama surprised me when she answered, "Nick brought a loaner over for you early this morning." When I quirked a questioning eyebrow at her, she continued, "I'm not supposed to tell you this, but when you mentioned that you'd have to wait and pay him once you get paid yourself, he decided to tackle a few other little jobs on your car. I know how he can underestimate the time those projects take, so I told him you might need a loner car in the interim."

I was simultaneously touched and horrified. How was I going to pay for even more repairs to my car? Mama must have recognized the look on my face, because she said quickly, "Keep in mind, Nick is doing these repairs in between his paying work. As a courtesy for taking Lucy to the haunted house."

I felt a lump in my throat as I said thank you.

The loaner car was parked at the side of the office, and I laughed heartily when Mama took me out there to show it to me. It was an old Cadillac that looked like some relic of the seventies, and it was one of the longest cars I had ever seen. I didn't know how I was going to drive it, let alone park it. There were some rusty spots in the camel-colored paint, and the passenger-side window didn't quite make it all the way to the top. Still, it was a car with a running engine, which was more than I could say for my car.

The drive to Barker Ranch only took fifteen minutes, and by the time I pulled off the two-lane road and onto the dirt driveway that led to the house, I felt like I had finally gotten the hang of keeping the giant Caddy in my own lane.

The ranch was on a breathtaking patch of land. The driveway sloped gently upward as I wound past a wild field on my right and a cow pasture on my left. The house itself was a two-story brick structure that sat right at the top of the hill. Before I got there, I passed a car that was pulled over on the grass between the driveway and the field. Leaning against the door was none other than the UFO hunter.

Without even stopping to think about what I was doing, I hit the brakes and killed the engine. I got out of the car and waved. "Hey, there! You're the UFO hunter, right? What's your name again?"

"Luke," the man answered, eyeing me warily. "Luke Dawes. I remember you from the diner."

"I'm Olivia. I was just coming out here to, ah, pay my condolences to Laurie. What about you?"

"I'm starting to get set up for the watch party."

"The UFO watch party? Is that still happening? I had figured, with Jared's murder and all…"

Luke shrugged. "I told Laurie we could cancel as long as she gave my rental fee back, but she said it was no problem to proceed. We'll have a moment of silence for Jared before we start."

Of course Laurie was allowing Luke to proceed, if she was getting money out of it. She would probably host a dozen UFO watch parties if it meant she could pay some bills.

"You want a tour?" Luke asked.

I really didn't, but to be polite, I said, "Sure."

Luke waved for me to follow him and hopped over the low wooden fence that led into the wild field. It wasn't quite as easy for me to make it over, but with a hand from Luke, I did. There was a beaten path to an old barn that leaned ever so slightly. Luke walked right through the gaping open doors and gestured around. "Jared's dad used to grow his own hay in that field, and this is where they would store it. Don't you love that smell?"

Frankly, it just smelled like old, dry hay, but I nodded affably as I looked around. The barn was still filled with tools and equipment, like it was just waiting for a farmer to come in and get to work.

"Come on," Luke said, waving his arm. He stepped through a side door of the barn, then turned to look at me as I followed. I gasped at the view. The barn had been built

107

right at the edge of the hilltop, and the land outside the side door fell away steeply. The sky beyond seemed gigantic, not stopping until it ran into a mountain range in the distance.

"Wow," I said. I hadn't been able to get excited about the smell of hay, but this view had been worth the drive.

"This is where we set up for the viewing party," Luke explained. "It's a great vantage point for seeing the ships that enter the atmosphere from the northwest. That's a common travel corridor for visitors."

"Interesting," I said. I couldn't believe I was having a casual chat with someone about the travel routes of aliens.

Luke pointed to the corner of the field that was closest to us. There were small green plants growing in neat rows there. "I planted moonflower. The flowers look like stars, and these will eventually grow up to be beautiful vines!"

"You're a farmer *and* a UFO hunter?" I asked.

"Oh, I'm no farmer. I just thought it would be fun to have a space-themed plant growing by the viewing area. Jared said he wasn't using the field, so I was welcome to plant in it."

Luke was even quirkier than I had originally thought, but I was honest when I said, "I appreciate the theming. Well done. I'm going to head on up to the house to see Laurie, but thanks for the tour."

As I turned to go, Luke shouted after me. "Tonight! Come join us!"

I drove up to the house, parked, and walked to the front door, then realized I wasn't even sure how to start this conversation. Was I supposed to offer my condolences again before I started asking Laurie about her late husband's connections?

I knocked, telling myself I would figure it out as I went.

Laurie answered the door, wearing a pretty floral sundress and strappy yellow sandals. She did not look like a woman in mourning. She laughed uncomfortably when she recognized me. "Did you enjoy our chat at the saloon so much that you're back for more?"

"Kind of," I admitted. Okay, this was an angle I could work with. "I thought maybe I could offer my condolences now that we're both sober."

Laurie stepped back and opened the door wider. "Come on in. You want some coffee?"

In short order, I was seated in Laurie and Jared's gorgeous living room, which had sliding glass doors that led onto a wide back porch with that same view I had gotten from the barn. Laurie put a cup of black coffee down in front of me. "I'm out of milk, I'm afraid."

"No problem." I decided to dive right in. "I realize we don't know each other, but considering that I… well, that I'm the one who—"

"Found him," Laurie supplied bluntly.

"Yeah. I guess I just feel like I have a sort of connection to all of this, and I'm anxious to help however I can."

Laurie had brought out a cup of coffee for herself, and she leaned back in the overstuffed recliner she had settled onto. "I'm overwhelmed with help. My parents, my sister, and my brother-in-law have been staying here since Wednesday, and Jared's family comes by every five minutes. I sent my family off to see the gunfight today. I needed some peace and quiet."

"When I said help, I meant as in finding out who killed your husband."

Laurie sat up straight, her coffee nearly sloshing over the rim of her cup. "Do you not trust the police to do it?"

The police don't know Jared might have been mauled by a were-wolf, I thought.

"Of course I do," I said quickly. "But this is a small town, right? I'm sure the police don't deal with this kind of thing often. I figured I could talk to people around town, maybe learn a few things that I could pass along to them."

Even as I said that, I wondered if the group at the Sanctuary would take any evidence against Zach to the police, or if they had their own ways of dealing with people who did bad things. I suspected the latter.

Laurie put her cup down on the coffee table between us and spread her hands. "Jared was a popular guy in this town. He still hung out with people he went to high school with, and he was respected by the community. I can't think of a single person who would have had it out for him."

"You're not from Nightmare, right?"

"No. Jared and I met in college. We got married right after graduation and moved here."

"Was it strange coming to a little town like this, where everybody already knows everybody else?"

Laurie snorted. "You have no idea. I practically needed an Excel spreadsheet just to keep track of all the connections, who can't be invited to the same barbecue because of a childhood grudge, or which families are still feuding over some generations-old dispute. It's ridiculous how long people here hold onto things. Now that Jared is gone, I'm going to sell this place to Emmett and get out as fast as I can."

"You really are going to sell the ranch, then?" I asked.

"Absolutely. Emmett has plans to build luxury rental cabins on this land, and he's made a good offer." Laurie gestured toward the sliding glass doors. "With views like this, it will be hugely popular."

I took a sip of coffee while pondering Laurie's words. Emmett's plans sounded like something that could be really lucrative, so I could see why he had been frustrated by Jared's reluctance to sell the ranch. Laurie, obviously, was a lot more willing to strike a deal. But if Emmett had killed Jared to get him out of the way, that still didn't explain why Jared's body had been covered in claw marks. Had Emmett hired Zach as a hit man? But that would mean Emmett knew what Zach was, and Gunnar had made it sound like the Sanctuary family kept their secret pretty well.

"Of course," Laurie continued in an offhand way, "converting this place from a ranch to rental cabins means no one has to worry about any more cows dying."

"You mentioned that at the saloon. You said it was weird how they died, but weird how?" Trying to lighten the mood, I winked at Laurie and said, "Should I be worried about eating the local steak?"

Laurie laughed half-heartedly. "I made fun of Jared for thinking aliens might have killed them, but my own theory is just as silly. Each time Jared found a dead cow in the pasture, it was almost drained of blood."

I coughed as my sip of coffee stuck in my throat. "Let me guess: there were big claw marks?"

"No. There were a few small claw marks, but that's not what did those cows in. What killed them was a tiny injury that was a lot more mysterious than scratches. Just two little spots on the neck, like a vampire had snuck into the pasture and sucked the blood from a cow."

CHAPTER SEVENTEEN

Laurie threw back her head and laughed while I just stared at her. As her mirth subsided, she reached up and wiped a tear from her eye. "It feels good to laugh like that. This has been an awful week, but at least my stupid vampire theory can still make me smile."

I tried to laugh in response, but I could hear how false and nervous I sounded. Mentally, I was flailing my arms and screaming. Laurie had no idea her theory might be right on the money. Was Mori responsible for killing the cattle? Was she sneaking out to the ranch to grab a meal now and then?

I hadn't even thought about the fact that if Mori was a real vampire, then she had to be getting blood from somewhere. She had been so nice to me, but was she leaving bodies—human, cow, or otherwise—all over Nightmare and its surrounding area?

"Anyway," Laurie said, "it hasn't happened in a few months. I had told Jared the aliens must have found a different ranch to visit. Speaking of aliens"—Laurie glanced in the direction of the field and lowered her voice, even though we were alone in the house—"I've also wondered if Luke killed those cows. Who knows what kind of weird things he's doing out there? I still can't believe Jared ever agreed to rent our land to him."

"You're still letting him have his UFO watch party tonight," I pointed out.

"Of course I am. I've got tomorrow's funeral to pay for!"

I had been right about that, at least. Laurie was desperate for the money.

There were a lot of questions surrounding the motives for Jared's murder, but all signs seemed to point to Emmett. No matter what, the real estate agent's name always came up. Even if Zach had actually done the killing, it seemed like Emmett might have been the one who ordered it.

I wrapped up my conversation with Laurie, and by the time I had climbed back into the hulking Caddy, I had made up my mind that I wanted to go to the UFO watch party that night. It might be a good way to speak to other locals and find out if Jared did, in fact, have enemies. Plus, I figured, maybe Mori would show up for a midnight cow snack, and I would catch her in the act.

On my way back down the driveway, I stopped again by Luke's car and went in search of him. He was busy arranging folding chairs on the far side of the barn, meticulously lining them up so they offered a perfect view of the northwest horizon. When I told him I was interested in coming to the watch party, he practically bounced on the balls of his feet in delight. "Wonderful! You're going to love it! Make sure you bring some warm layers, and don't forget your bug spray!"

I promised I would come prepared, and I wondered about my strange new life during my entire drive back to the motel. I was going to work at a haunted house in the evening, then attend a UFO viewing party afterward. I was so far out of my comfort zone, and yet, strangely, it somehow felt perfectly normal here in the town of Nightmare.

"Who knows?" I mused out loud. "Maybe I'll even see a UFO!"

Despite having a car, I still decided to walk to the Lusty Lunch Counter for my daily cheeseburger and fries. Ella was on duty again, and I filled her in on my plans for the evening. She just laughed and wished me good luck. "You're getting good at hanging out with this town's strangest people," she said.

"At least it keeps things interesting," I countered, waving a french fry.

Instead of avoiding all the tourists on my walk back to the motel, I went right down High Noon Boulevard. The covered boardwalk offered shade from the sun, and now that I was over my surprise by the touristy, tacky little street, I just let myself relax and enjoy it. I didn't feel the need to buy myself an overpriced cowboy hat, but it was entertaining to watch the costumed actors who were roaming around.

My walk back from lunch was followed by a lazy afternoon that included a short nap, but by the time I set out for work that evening, I had a growing feeling of trepidation. My suspicions about Mori meant I would either have to try to play it cool with her or outright ask her if she was a cow-sucking vampire. Talk about an awkward subject.

I drove to the Sanctuary and parked in a far corner of the grass lot where a few other cars already were. I just figured that was the employee parking lot. When I reached the front doors, I stopped and took a deep breath, telling myself Mori was my friend, and I could trust her not to come after my neck if I confronted her about the cows.

"Olivia," a man's voice said.

I looked to my right and saw Zach at the ticket window, and I felt a chill run through me. The last time I had seen the guy, he was covered in fur and chasing after someone. "Zach," I said.

Zach paused, and when I didn't say anything else, he said, "Come here."

Had he seen me? I wondered. *Does he know that I know?*

My arms were stiff at my sides as I stopped at the ticket window. "What?" I asked.

Zach reached forward with one arm, and I flinched. "What's with you?" he growled. "You're on edge today."

I looked down and saw that Zach was holding a white envelope with my name written on it. I just stared at it, until Zach raised his arm and waved it in front of my face. "It's your pay. Take it."

"Oh." I plucked the envelope out of his hand. "Thanks."

Okay, so I had panicked for nothing. I felt silly as I walked to the locker room, and I had to force myself to relax. By the time I made it to the dining room for the evening's family meeting, I was practically shaking from nerves. My fear that Zach knew I had witnessed his transformation had put me on edge.

Mori gave me a wave from her spot at our usual table. My shoulders instantly tensed up. By the time I sat down on the bench opposite Mori, I felt like my entire body was taut.

"You look a little nervous," Mori said in greeting.

"Oh, do I?" I tried to say it casually, but of course, it came out sounding stiff and uncomfortable.

"It's okay," Mori said, leaning forward and putting a hand over mine. She had done that once before, and I had noticed how cool her touch was. Now, I knew it was because she was undead.

Undead. I swallowed hard. It was like I had been in shock up until this point, and it was wearing off at last. The reality that I was sitting in a room surrounded by creatures I had never even believed existed was sinking in. They were supernatural, and they were dangerous.

"It's okay," Mori said again, her voice more firm. "Look at me, Olivia. I know that you know."

My heart seemed to lurch in my chest as visions of cows ran through my head. "How do you know? I haven't even said anything yet!" *Is she reading my mind?*

Mori's eyebrows drew together. "Gunnar told me what you two experienced last night. He said that once you knew what Zach was, you realized all of us are exactly who we are every night in our vignettes. You're clever, so I wasn't surprised you figured it out so quickly."

"Right!" I said as relief flooded through me. Could vampires even read minds? I wasn't sure.

"Now, you just mentioned you hadn't said anything yet. About what?" Mori asked.

I sighed. It was time to just put it out there, but I was still too timid to dive right in. "Mori, I was wondering…" *Oh, boy, this is uncomfortable.* "That is, if you're a vampire, then you drink blood, right?"

"Of course."

"Well, where do you get it?"

Mori leaned back, finally moving her hand away from mine. Her smile was teasing. "Are you worried I'm going to come after you for a little snack when I have my break tonight?"

I had considered that possibility, but I didn't want to admit it. "Should I be worried?"

Mori laughed, and her tone returned to a gentle, reassuring one. "I feed off tourists. I mesmerize them so they won't remember anything, drink enough to satisfy my craving but not enough to kill them, then send them on their way. Everyone tastes different, you know. So by drinking from a different tourist every time, I get a great variety of flavors. They go home with a strange little mark on their neck, figuring they must have stumbled into something after a long night at the saloon. No one is the wiser."

I wasn't sure if Mori drinking the blood of tourists was better or worse than the idea of her going after cattle, but at least she wasn't killing them. "So," I said hesitantly, "you're not drinking cow blood, then?"

Mori's mouth shrank to a thin line, and she sat up stiffly. "What makes you ask that?"

"I talked to Jared's widow today," I admitted. "She said that a few of their cows had died. They were found drained of blood, with puncture wounds at their necks."

One of my hands was resting on the bench, and I felt a little tickle at my fingers. I shook my hand to fling off what I figured was just a bug.

"Are you asking me if I killed those cows?" Mori asked.

"Are there any other vampires in town who might have done it?" Again, I felt something against my fingers, but this time it was sharper. "Ow!" I cried, looking down. Mori's little pet was under the table, and it was nibbling on my fingertips. As I looked at it, the creature seemed to smile at me, and I saw two little fangs gleaming against its gray skin.

I looked up at Mori. "That is not a dog."

Mori sighed. "No, of course not. He's a chupacabra, and *he* drinks cow blood."

CHAPTER EIGHTEEN

"After Baxter disappeared," Mori said, "Felipe developed some behavioral problems. Chupacabras are very sensitive creatures, you know, and he felt Baxter's absence as strongly as the rest of us."

I glanced down at the thing that was still nibbling at my hand. "You have a pet chupacabra named Felipe," I said in disbelief. I pulled my fingers away and wiped them on my jeans. *Chupacabra spit. Ew.*

"He's named after a former lover," Mori said. "Anyway, Felipe got loose a few times in the wake of Baxter's disappearance, and all three times, we found him at Barker Ranch. I hated it for Jared. He didn't deserve to lose those cows, but I couldn't tell him the truth of what had happened."

"Gunnar never said it outright, but I got the impression Nightmare's supernatural residents aren't open about their, uh, status."

"Certainly not. There are three different communities in Nightmare. You've got the regular town residents, those of us who are supernatural, and the tourists who come and go. All three of those communities exist in overlapping but separate worlds. There are only a handful of them who know about us, and we make sure they keep the secret."

Mori paused, and I looked down at Felipe again. He

was now scrabbling at my shoes with his front paws. It was hard to believe the little thing was responsible for so much destruction at Barker Ranch.

"He actually prefers goat blood, you know," Mori said casually, noticing my attention had returned to Felipe. "There aren't a lot of those in this town, so he had to turn to cattle."

"What does he drink when he isn't loose?"

"Don't worry. I have a deal with the butcher. Normally, his meals are ethically sourced."

"Jared's widow said it looked like a vampire attack, so she wasn't far off the mark."

"Jared himself was going all over Nightmare, telling anyone who would listen what had happened. A lot of folks thought his story sounded ridiculous, of course, but there are some smart people in this town who are paying attention. People we wouldn't want knowing the truth."

Justine was making her way to the podium, and Mori and I both fell silent. I didn't actually hear a word Justine said. I was too busy going over every little detail of the conversation in my mind. I was relieved to know Mori wasn't responsible for the drained cattle, but it was unnerving to think her pet chupacabra was.

Pet chupacabra. The idea was so ridiculous I nearly laughed out loud. It seemed like some kind of joke, and I wouldn't have believed it if Felipe wasn't right there at my feet. He had, at least, finally settled down, and he was now curled up under the table.

Unfortunately for Mori, I still had my suspicions about her. If Jared had been telling everyone about his cows, then she might have gotten nervous that someone would connect the dots and come after her and Felipe. I still thought it was entirely possible she had killed Jared to shut him up. Maybe she had even staged the claw marks somehow to frame Zach.

I hated having such dark thoughts about someone who had been so nice to me, but I wasn't giving anyone a free pass. Until the killer was caught and my job was secure, I was going to consider every possible lead.

My attention snapped back to the present when I heard Justine say my name. "You'll be in the lagoon vignette, with the pirates," she was saying. "Head to wardrobe after this, and they'll get you squared away."

I didn't even know there was a wardrobe room, let alone where it was. As soon as Justine dismissed everyone, I asked Mori for directions, and she pointed me to a room just a few doors down, adding, "Have fun and be scary!"

The wardrobe room was a cavernous space filled with rolling clothing racks. Every single one was packed with costumes. Rubber monster heads of various types were arranged on shelves along one wall, and near the back was a long table with makeup mirrors and lights. As I watched, a woman sitting in front of one of the mirrors meticulously painted an infected-looking cut onto her cheek.

A short man with slicked-back black hair and a mustache approached me. "Olivia," he said without a trace of doubt. "I have your costume over here. Follow me."

The man led me to a rack on one side of the room, selected a hanger, and presented the costume on it with a flourish. "There are changing spaces behind you, and I'll have the boots waiting for you when you get out."

Just a few minutes later, I emerged from the small changing room, wearing a long red velvet skirt with a matching coat and a black shirt that had lace at the cuffs. I had cinched a brown leather corset belt over the coat, and there was a plethora of accessories hanging from it on straps, including a compass, a pistol, and a miniature tele-scope. A black tricorn pirate hat sat jauntily on my head. I had to admit, it was really fun to play dress up like this.

The mustached man was waiting for me, as promised,

and he handed me a pair of tall brown leather boots that folded over at the top. Once I had wiggled my feet and calves into them, he pointed me toward the makeup tables. "Pin your hair up so it will go under your hat, put on extra eye makeup to look a little wild, and add some red lipstick. You're going to be a fabulous pirate!"

I did as instructed, and by the time I made my way to what Justine had called the lagoon vignette, I was excited about getting to be a part of the show that night. As soon as I walked into the space, Theo sidled up to me. "I'm not actually a zombie, you know," he said conversationally.

Apparently, everyone had been informed that I knew the secret of the Sanctuary. Somehow, that didn't surprise me. I laughed and said, "I figured, since I've seen you without all this zombie makeup. But if everyone else here really is what they pretended to be, then why are you just playing a part?"

"I actually was a pirate!" Theo grinned at me. "I'm also a vampire, but as you can see, I lost my fangs, so playing a vampire isn't an option. I do the zombie routine because it's much scarier than being a regular old pirate."

"How did you lose your fangs?" I narrowed my eyes and peered at Theo in the lights from overhead. His teeth were white and gleaming, so I didn't think it was something as basic as cavities.

Theo's grin disappeared. "Oh, it's a long story. Anyway, let me give you the rundown." Theo walked me through the scene, detailing where everyone's space was. He positioned me near the exit of the room. "Your job," he said solemnly, "is to make sure guests don't linger too long. In other words, chase them out. Move in close behind them, and they'll get nervous and speed up. Or, if that doesn't work, tell them you'll make them walk the plank if they don't move along."

"So I'm a spooky pirate bouncer," I said. I could do that.

No sooner had I spoken than the lights overhead flashed three times in quick succession, then went out entirely, leaving only the ambient lighting that set the scene so well. "That means the first guests are entering the Sanctuary," Theo told me. He winked. "Have fun, and grab me if you need anything!"

Just a few minutes later, a group of five people, huddled together and giggling, came into the room. I was so busy watching Theo, the siren, and the other pirates that I almost forgot to jump into action when the people came past me. I turned and followed them, and the young woman in the back looked over her shoulder, shrieked, and began herding her group into the next vignette.

I felt silly the first few times I threatened guests with walking the plank, but eventually, I settled into the role and really started having fun with it. The hardest part of the whole evening was trying not to stare at the siren. She spent a lot of her time under the water in her glass-fronted tank, and it was utterly fascinating to me. I overheard guests saying what a realistic mermaid she was, and all I could think was, "Honey, you have no idea."

Honestly, it felt kind of good to be in on the Sanctuary's secret. I felt like I was part of an elite club or something. I knew the truth, and the hundreds of people filing past me all night long didn't. I felt special.

I tried to think of a time I had felt that way during all my years in Nashville, but I couldn't.

I had just chased off a middle-aged couple when a hand grabbed my arm. I yelped and turned to see Clara's face peeking through a door I hadn't even known was there. It was painted black, like the walls, and the handle was the same color. It was wonderfully camouflaged. "Break time!" she said in a loud whisper. "Come on!"

Clara waved me through the door, shut it quickly behind me, and led me through a maze of narrow tunnels that I guessed wound between all the various scenes. There were doors every so often with the name of the scene they led to written on them, and as we walked, I could hear the shrieks and screams of guests.

It was a good thing Clara was leading me, because I never would have found my way to the east wing on my own. If there wasn't a map of those tunnels, then it was going to take me a while to learn my way around them. Eventually, though, I was seated in the dining room. I was sure I looked funny, dressed as a pirate while chowing down on potato chips and cookies.

Someone plunked a heavy, leather-bound book down on the table next to me, and I looked up to see Madge, the middle witch. She tossed her curls over her shoulder and said, "May I join you? I'd like to show you something."

"Of course," I said, curious. It was the first time I had seen one of the witches without the other two, and I was mildly surprised they ever split up. I guess I had assumed they traveled in a pack all the time.

Madge sat down smoothly and put a hand on the cover of the book. "This is a photo album that shows the Sanctuary over the past forty years or so. Now that you know about us, I thought you might enjoy seeing how this place has changed over the years." She opened the album to the first page, and I saw a faded photo of a smiling man standing in front of the building. He looked like he was middle aged, and he was wearing a purple top hat.

"That's Baxter," Madge explained. She began to turn the pages slowly, showing me how the different vignettes had changed over the years and pointing out some of the people who were still working at the Sanctuary. "There's Theo! He's been playing a pirate for at least thirty years now!"

Madge turned the page again, and I saw a group of five young men, probably just teenagers, standing proudly behind a row of headstones. "Those boys made most of what you see in the graveyard vignette," Madge said proudly. "The headstones are carved out of foam, and they did such a great job making them look real."

My hand shot out when Madge began to turn the page. "Wait!" I said, my fingers wrapping lightly around her wrist. I leaned closer to the photo and pointed at one of the teenagers. "That's Damien." He was much younger, and he had been a little gangly back then, but there was no mistaking that it was Baxter's son in the photo.

"Yes. And there's Zach." Madge pointed to a boy who stood slightly apart from the others, not smiling but still looking proud of his handiwork.

"Who are the others? Do they still work here, too?"

Madge pointed to one of them. "He moved east." Her finger hovered over another, as if she didn't want to touch the image. "That one went bad. He's not here anymore."

"And the boy next to Damien?"

"Oh. That's Jared Barker. He and Damien were best friends back then."

CHAPTER NINETEEN

I rested my elbow on the table and propped my chin in my hand, staring hard at the photo. My head felt like it was spinning from Madge's revelation. I wouldn't have recognized this young Jared Barker on my own.

I blew out the breath I realized I was holding. "Are they still friends? Er, were they, before Jared's murder?"

"No. This was a long time ago." Madge's voice was sad. "Something happened between them, not long after this photo was taken. They became enemies. Jared stopped coming here, and Damien, well, you've met him. You know how he is. He wasn't like that before his rift with Jared."

Alarm bells were going off in my head. Was it really a coincidence that Damien had arrived in Nightmare to "save" the Sanctuary just two days after Jared's murder? Had he actually arrived earlier and murdered his former friend? If he really wanted an excuse to close the haunt, staging a murder on our front doorstep would certainly work.

"What happened to ruin their friendship?" I asked.

Madge shook her head slowly. "I don't know. I'm not sure anyone here does. Damien would never talk about it. After that, all he wanted to do was get away from this life and this town." Madge closed the book with force, like she was trying to shut out the unsettling history between

Damien and Jared. She seemed to realize I was finished with the trip down memory lane, and she stood. "Maybe this information will be helpful," she said, looking at me significantly.

"Has anyone told the police about their relationship?"

"Perhaps, but does it matter? They're probably going to decide Jared was killed by a wild animal."

I watched as Madge walked away, then my eyes flicked up to the clock above the door. My break was nearly over, and I hadn't finished my cookies yet. I scarfed them down even as I stood and walked back to the entrance to the network of paths between the vignettes.

I only got lost twice before I finally cracked open the door that led to my spot in the lagoon.

During the lulls between guests coming through, I considered that wild animal angle. Every suspect in Jared's murder—Emmett, Mori, Damien, even Laurie—seemed unlikely. The claw marks had been made by something bigger than Felipe, and unless one of them was secretly a werewolf, then the evidence continued pointing to Zach.

Of course, that led right back to the theory that Zach might have been hired by someone. He was in that photo with Damien and Jared, which meant they had all known each other for a long time. Had Damien hired Zach as a hit man to nudge the Sanctuary closer to its demise?

Clearly, I needed to get more information from Zach. Gunnar had been against it, thinking it was too dangerous, but I was getting too impatient to care.

When the Sanctuary finally closed for the night, the lights blinked three times again, then turned on completely. "And we're done for the night!" Theo told me. "Great job, Olivia. You really fit in here."

Again, there was someone telling me I belonged. It felt good, like it was filling up some part of me I hadn't even realized was empty.

There was a crowd of people in the wardrobe room, so I chatted with Theo while we waited for a turn to get changed out of our costumes. Even once I was back in my regular clothes, though, that still left me with a face full of makeup I would never wear out into the real world. *At least*, I told myself, *it's dark outside.*

I said my goodbyes and wasted no time driving back to the motel. I had a UFO watch party to get to. Once I was back in my room, I washed my face, put on moisturizer, and called it good. There was no point in putting on my regular—and much less dramatic—makeup just to go sit in a dark field.

The Cadillac had one headlight out, so it was a dark drive out to Barker Ranch. Those twisty roads through the hills were fine during the day, but driving on them in the wee hours of the morning made me a bit nervous. By the time I pulled into the dirt driveway of the ranch, I could tell my fingers were practically glued to the steering wheel.

There was a line of cars pulled to the side of the drive, so I nosed in behind the last one and turned off the car. I had brought a sweatshirt with me, and when I stepped out, I was grateful Luke had reminded me to bring layers. It was downright chilly so far out from the town.

I made my way to the far side of the barn without too much stumbling and swearing, and I told myself that if I ever did this again, I would bring a flashlight, too. When I rounded the corner of the barn, I saw a group of about twenty people sitting on lawn chairs, chatting quietly while gazing at the sky. Someone had a telescope set up, too.

As I got closer, one of those people stood up, and I recognized Luke's voice before I could really see his face. "Olivia, welcome! Here, I have a chair and a blanket for you." In short order, I was seated next to Luke, a wool blanket draped over my legs.

Luke brandished a pair of binoculars. "Let me know if you want to borrow these."

"Thank you. In the meantime, I'm happy to sit here and appreciate this gorgeous night sky. I haven't been in a place this dark for years. I forgot how many stars you can see."

There was real affection in Luke's voice when he replied, "Yeah, it's spectacular out here. It's easy to understand why Jared wasn't willing to give this place up, isn't it?"

I looked at Luke. "I heard Jared and Emmett arguing at the Lusty Lunch Counter last Saturday. Jared was firm that he didn't want to make a deal, but I don't think his reason for refusing was the great view."

Luke made a noise that might have been a laugh or a sigh. "Yeah, he was awfully attached to the idea of being a cattle rancher. He wanted to be just like his dad."

Someone to Luke's left began talking to him, so I sat back and focused my gaze on the night sky. Eventually, as the minutes slipped by, my brain began to slow down a little. I didn't expect to see a UFO, of course, but I had been honest when I told Luke it was beautiful. Watching the stars twinkle overhead was a perfect way to relax.

I wasn't sure how much time went by before I heard the sound of footsteps. I didn't pay attention to them until Luke perked up next to me and said happily, "Zach! You made it! I'll get you a chair!"

Don't look, don't look, don't look, I told myself.

Too late. My head was already turning in Zach's direction.

And then, to make it even worse, Luke plunked a lawn chair down right next to me. I muttered a weak "hey" as Zach sat down, but I shouldn't have bothered, since he didn't even acknowledge my presence.

I was surprised, then, when Zach said a few minutes

later, "I figured I'd be the only one from the Sanctuary out here."

"I met Luke in town last week, and he invited me," I answered.

"Do you believe in UFOs?"

"No, but I'm willing to be open minded. How about you?"

"They could exist. Who knows? There are plenty of strange things here on our own planet that most people don't believe in." Even in the dark, I could tell Zach was giving me a sly look.

"Good point," I said. Zach making small talk with me was possibly more shocking than an actual UFO would be. I couldn't imagine what had merited this change in his demeanor.

We continued to make occasional conversation, and I nearly pinched myself to make sure I wasn't dreaming the whole thing. I had just checked my watch to see it was already two o'clock in the morning when someone moved to stand at the front of our group. I heard Laurie say, "Hello, UFO hunters! I brought out some hot cocoa, so I'll be coming around with that for you."

Apparently, Laurie really, really wanted to keep Luke and his group happy, even when I knew she would be up early the next morning to get ready for her husband's funeral.

When Laurie made it over to me, she greeted me warmly and handed me a Styrofoam cup. Then her glance fell on Zach, and her expression clouded over. "Zach, how nice to see you here," she said. The smile returned to her face, but it was ridiculously fake, as was the high-pitched, friendly tone. Zach just nodded in response, then declined a cup of cocoa.

Zach didn't say another word as Laurie continued her rounds. His earlier friendliness had disappeared. When

Laurie began to walk back toward the house, Zach got up and followed her, circling around the back of the group.

I could barely see Zach catch up to Laurie. The moon had already set, so only the starlight illuminated their forms. Their heads were so close together I figured they were whispering to each other. Both of them began to gesture, their movements becoming bigger and more exaggerated as their conversation continued.

I felt an overwhelming sense of déjà vu. It looked an awful lot like what I had witnessed in the alley behind the saloon.

Finally, the conversation at an end, Laurie continued on her way, and Zach returned to his seat. He sat stiffly and stared straight ahead. Quietly, almost too low for me to hear, he said, "I know what you're thinking."

"No, you don't," I said, slightly defensively.

"You think I killed Jared."

Oh, wow, so Zach actually knows exactly what I'm thinking.

When I didn't answer, he continued, "Just like everyone else. And you probably think I'm going to kill Laurie next. I got rid of Jared, and now I'm going to get rid of his widow."

"Actually, I wasn't thinking that. Although you and Laurie did seem to be having a heated discussion just now, exactly like on Thursday night."

Zach looked at me sharply. "What are you talking about?"

Oops. It had just slipped out. I cleared my throat to buy myself some time. "Last night... Gunnar and I... Well, you know, Under the Undertaker's is off that alley..."

Zach actually laughed. "That's how you learned the secret of the Sanctuary, isn't it? You saw me change."

"Yeah." There was no point denying it.

"No wonder you were looking so tense tonight. I

thought you were just trying to process our existence, but you were worried about me, too, weren't you?"

I nodded.

"Olivia, I'm not trying to hurt Laurie. I'm trying to help her."

CHAPTER TWENTY

"It sure didn't look like you were trying to help her in the alley last night," I told Zach.

"I know. I got angry. Believe it or not, I'm Laurie's accountant."

I burst out laughing. When Zach just continued to gaze at me stoically, I calmed down and said, "Wait, really?"

"I don't know why that's so funny," Zach said in an affronted tone.

"You're a werewolf accountant who works at a haunted house. It's kind of funny."

Zach growled quietly. "I guess I can see that. I grew up here, but I went to college in Phoenix and got my accounting degree."

"What brought you back?"

"The Sanctuary. I got a job in Phoenix after I graduated, but calling in sick three days every month started looking suspicious really quickly. Plus, I was living in a big city, where I couldn't just roam freely during the full moon. I realized I felt too vulnerable out in the real world. I needed the safety of the Sanctuary, and I needed to be in a place where I could be myself."

"You don't have to hide what you are those three nights a month," I said, nodding. "In fact, you're able to put yourself on display, and no one is the wiser."

"Yeah. And on top of working the ticket window and doing security, I also do accounting for the Sanctuary. Laurie came to me and asked me to get the finances for Barker Ranch in order, too. Jared wasn't much of a businessman."

Something about the way Zach worded his story caught my attention. "Let me guess: Jared didn't know you were cleaning up his financial mess?"

"Laurie wanted to keep my involvement a secret, because she knew it would upset Jared. I was meeting with her when Jared's body was dumped at the Sanctuary. And I've been refusing to tell anyone why I wasn't on security duty that day, because saying I was with the murder victim's wife at the time would only make me look even more suspicious."

"But you'd have an alibi," I interjected.

"Can you tell me the exact time Jared was killed?"

"Of course not."

"Exactly. And I only met with Laurie for an hour. I could have been with her, then killed Jared, or vice versa. I saw the cop cars heading to the Sanctuary while I was on my way back there, and I panicked. I snuck though the trees to see what was happening, but I was too scared to come out of hiding. Telling the truth will only complicate things for me."

I had to concede that Zach had a point. "What happened last night then? I heard you on the phone, and it sounded like you didn't want to have that meeting in the alley."

"Of course I didn't. Laurie still wanted my help. Even though she'll be able to sell the ranch without Jared getting in the way, she still needs to get their finances sorted out. Jared had claw marks in his chest, so I knew someone wanted to make me look guilty. I worried how much more guilty I would seem if anyone caught me meeting with

Laurie again. And, of course, I was caught, by you and Gunnar."

"Then why did you agree to meet her?"

Zach sighed. "After everything I did for her, she threatened to expose me if I quit helping her."

I grasped the arms of my chair. "So even before you transformed last night, Laurie already knew the truth?"

"No, of course not! I mean she was going to expose that I was doing the ranch's accounting in secret. She figured that if I wouldn't help her anymore, she'd just make me look guilty. She knows Jared and I have a… difficult past."

Here we go! I thought. I was about to get some juicy details that might just put Damien in the top suspect slot. I knew Zach could feel the curiosity practically oozing from me as I said, "I did see a photo today of you, Jared, and Damien. I hadn't realized you were all friends once."

"You can't tell by the way he treats me these days, but Damien saved my life when I was a teenager."

Okay, that was not the dirt I had been expecting to get. In fact, it wasn't dirt at all. "Don't tell me that jerk is actually a good guy," I said bitterly.

"He used to be a good guy, at any rate. Jared and I were never close friends. We just both happened to be friends with Damien, so we moved in the same circle. As we got older, the fact that I was different than the other kids became more obvious. My school absences during the full moon, my injuries from running wild in my wolf form… Jared didn't know I was a werewolf, but he knew I didn't fit in, and he started to bully me. It got worse as we got older."

"Oh, Zach, I'm so sorry," I said sincerely. Here I had been so intimidated by Zach and thought he was such a grumpy jerk, and now I was feeling sorry for him.

"Jared took it too far one night. He and some other

boys ganged up on me. Damien found us and got me out of there. It ruined his relationship with his normal friends. You know, the friends who weren't part of the Sanctuary."

"Madge did say that Damien seemed to change not long after that photo was taken. Damien resented losing that part of his world, didn't he?"

"Yes. Plus, he and his dad had some kind of falling out. None of us know what it was about. Damien left town the day after he graduated high school. Monday night was the first time I'd seen him since we got our diplomas."

"And then he only showed up to threaten us and tell us what irresponsible losers we are," I supplied.

"That's why Damien's speech the other day made me so mad. He knows I'm the one doing the accounting for the Sanctuary, and he also knows that I've been doing it for years without any problems, but he hates the place and wants any excuse to close it."

"Is the Sanctuary really in as much financial trouble as Damien implied?"

"It's not great," Zach admitted. "It's not through anybody's fault, though. Part of the building had to be renovated, then there was an electrical short that caused a small fire. It's like we've had a run of bad luck ever since Baxter left. Maybe bad luck isn't the right term for it. It's like the old hospital building is beginning to crumble without him there to watch over it."

We both fell silent for a few moments. It wasn't an uncomfortable silence. Rather, I could tell we were both processing everything that had just been said.

"Zach," I finally said. "You've been short and, some-times, downright rude to me since we met. Why the sudden change tonight?"

Zach looked at me for a long time, his gaze surprisingly soft. Almost, I thought, sympathetic. "When you showed up for your interview," he said, "I thought you were just some normal person, an outsider who couldn't be trusted. Look at Laurie. She found out what I am at the same time you did, and you saw how she treated me tonight. She's terrified but also convinced she only imagined me transforming. You and I, on the other hand, are getting along just fine. You've already accepted me for who I am. The more I've seen of you, the more I'm convinced that you belong at the Sanctuary. You fit in with us because you don't fit in anywhere else."

By this point, I was getting used to hearing that. Coming from someone as standoffish as Zach, though, it seemed to carry even more weight. "We'll see," I told him.

The other UFO watchers started to pack up and leave about half an hour later. I could hear the yawns from the people around me, and I realized I was utterly exhausted. I said good night to Zach and Luke, then drove back to the motel with the radio blaring to help me stay alert.

It wasn't until I woke up Saturday morning that I remembered the envelope Zach had handed me. I looked inside it and found a stack of cash. I had never discussed pay with Justine, and the amount was a pleasant surprise. I had made enough to pay Mama for my week at the motel, and then some. There wasn't quite enough yet to pay for my car, but I set aside money for that plus money for food. I could, at least, expand my horizons beyond the Lusty Lunch Counter. One more paycheck, I figured, and I would be back on my way to San Diego.

When I walked into the motel office for my morning coffee, I was feeling good. I poured my coffee, then happily asked Mama what I owed her.

"About that," she said.

My heart sank. Did I owe more than I thought?

"You said you did marketing back in Nashville, right?" she continued.

I shook my head in confusion at the same time I tried to nod, so I was sure I looked just like a bobble-head toy.

"Well, this motel could use a little good publicity. We get a steady stream of customers, but I'm nowhere close to selling out, except on holiday weekends. If you agree to do a little marketing work for us during the rest of your stay, I'll give you half off what you owe me for the past week. And"—Mama held up her finger and grinned at me—"I won't charge you for the rest of your stay, however long that might be."

I nearly dropped my coffee cup in my excitement, and I agreed so quickly the words came out a tangled jumble. Mama just laughed and gave me a satisfied nod. "You'll be moving out of your room, though. There's an efficiency apartment at the back of the south wing. That and the upstairs of this office building were designed so property managers could live on site, but Benny and I needed more space than that, so we live about a mile down the road. You'll have to air the apartment out and spruce it up a bit, but it's clean and sunny."

Even if I was only in Nightmare for another week, I was grateful for the free stay. Well, not free, exactly, but I was happy to trade my marketing expertise for a small apartment.

And I did want to leave in just one more week. Didn't I?

I felt a strange sense of discomfort at the idea. In a week, I would not only have the car paid for, but, thanks to Mama's offer, I would have gas and food money to get to San Diego, and probably a bit left over after that.

I thought of Zach's words the night before, and how kindly he had looked at me when he told me I belonged at the Sanctuary. I realized my departure wouldn't be tied to money, after all. I was going to stay until Jared's murderer was found. It was the least I could do for my new friends.

Within an hour, I was plopping my suitcases down onto a very dusty rust-orange shag rug. The efficiency was small but cozy, and since it was on the second level, it had a much better view and more sun than my ground-floor room had. The kitchenette was basic but sufficient, and I was happy to see that the fridge and stove weren't as old as the rug. I was pretty sure it had been installed when plaid bell-bottoms were still in fashion.

There was a double bed in an alcove, and I sneezed when I whipped the sheet off it and a cloud of dust flew into the air. Cleaning was clearly my top priority. Mama had loaned me a vacuum, a mop, and spray cleaner, and I got to work as soon as I had opened up the windows to let in some fresh air.

By the time I finished cleaning and had new sheets on the bed, it was nearly time to leave for work. Still, my efforts had been worth it. The apartment no longer smelled like an antique store, and I had my clothes neatly arranged in a tall wooden dresser.

I took a quick shower, humming to myself while I washed my hair. It was only after I was dressed and putting on my shoes that I noticed a white sheet of paper on the floor, right in front of the door.

It was a note written in a thick, scrawling hand. Someone had shoved it under my door while I had been showering.

It read, *Leave town. Today.*

CHAPTER TWENTY-ONE

I ran out of the apartment so fast that I didn't even stop to put my shoes on. I regretted that the instant my bare feet hit the hot concrete at the bottom of the stairs, and I did a frog-like hop-run all the way from the back of the motel to the front office. By the time I banged open the office door, I was out of breath, and the soles of my feet felt like hot pins were being shoved into them.

"Ow! Mama! Help!" I cried as I hopped from one foot to the other.

I could see Mama's voluminous hair sticking up from behind the front desk, which meant she was sitting at the computer. She rose up with a look on her face that said she was ready to defend me or comfort me, depending on the nature of my distress.

"Are you hurt?" she asked sternly, eyeing my feet.

"No. But I ran up here barefooted. I'm too old for that." It was one thing to go without shoes at ten years old. It was another to do it in your forties. "But I just found this under my door. Did you see anyone suspicious go past the office?" I put the note on the counter and hopped backward, putting some distance between me and it.

Mama gazed at the note for a long time before she looked up at me, her mouth set in a firm line. "I didn't see anyone, but they could have approached from the alley behind the property. Do you think this has to do with Jared's murder?"

I nodded. There was no other explanation. Apparently, someone was paying attention to what I was doing, and one of my wild shots had actually hit close to the mark. What would happen if I didn't leave town? Would investigating Jared's murder lead to my own?

"I have to get out of town," I said in a rush. "Like this note says. But my car isn't ready, and the Caddy won't get me far. Plus, it's not even my car, and I don't have the money to buy it off of Nick. And if I leave, then I can't pay for my actual car, and then it's stuck here in Nightmare while I'm running away from all of this, and—"

"Olivia," Mama said in a commanding tone.

I instantly stopped rambling and looked at her, even as I felt tears welling in my eyes. *Don't cry, don't cry, don't cry,* I told myself. "Should I call the police?" I asked in a slightly less hysterical voice.

"Yes, of course you should." Mama was already picking up the phone. "Actually, I'll handle that. You sit and give your poor feet a break."

I dutifully complied, and twenty minutes later, the same police officer who had questioned me the night Jared's body had been discovered came through the door. Mama handed him the note and a cup of coffee, and then he sat down next to me.

There wasn't much for me to tell, and there really wasn't much the police could do. Officer Reyes explained to me that without any leads, my best bet was to simply stay vigilant and to alert the police if anything else happened.

"You know," Officer Reyes said, giving me a sideways glance before taking a long sip of coffee, "sometimes, new people aren't so welcome in Nightmare, especially people caught up in a murder investigation. Maybe someone took issue with the fact that you showed up out of nowhere, got a job with those weird folks at the haunted house, and *found*"—I couldn't help but notice the emphasis he put on that word, which was only missing the sarcastic air quotes —"the body of a beloved community member, all in your first three days here."

Okay, point taken. I conceded as much, and before leaving, Officer Reyes admonished me to stop running around town, asking questions about Jared and his relationships. I didn't bother to ask how he knew. In a small town like this, everyone probably knew.

Once it was just Mama and me again, I said, "I still have to decide whether to stick around and take my chances, or find a way out of here."

Mama made a noise of impatience. "You should stay. You're going to shake things up in this town, and, maybe, this town is going to shake you up a bit. Don't hightail it out of here just yet. Stick with what you started."

"It could be dangerous," I noted.

"I'll find someone to act as your own personal security guard tonight. By the time you're done with work, I'll have somebody waiting for you at the ticket window to escort you home. In the meantime, I'll have to do. I'm driving you to work."

I smiled, despite my fear. "Thanks, Mama." I glanced at the clock on the wall and yelped. "And we need to get going! I have to be there in six minutes!"

I dashed back to my apartment, sticking to the shadows as much as possible, and grabbed socks, shoes, and my purse. By the time I came back downstairs, Mama was out front in an old midnight-blue Mustang, the engine rumbling. I hopped in and put on my shoes while she drove.

It was exactly seven o'clock by the time I leaped out of the car in front of the old hospital building. I thanked

Mama, and she just pointed at me and said, "You don't go beyond that ticket window without your security guard."

That was a promise I would be happy to keep. I trusted Mama's judgment, so I knew she would find someone who could help keep me safe. I reminded myself that the note might be an empty threat, but it didn't hurt to take precautions.

It was difficult to chat casually with Mori and Theo as we waited in the dining room for the family meeting to begin. I was suddenly looking at everyone with suspicion. Had someone there shoved that note under my door? Had Zach simply been making small talk during the UFO watch party to throw suspicion off of himself? Even Mori was still on my list. Everyone at the Sanctuary kept telling me that I belonged, but maybe there was someone who disagreed.

I spied Damien standing at the back of the room while Justine addressed all of us from the podium. He was wearing his sunglasses again, which, of course, only made him look ridiculous. We were indoors. If the vampires could handle the overhead lights, then so could Damien.

Maybe Damien had put that note under my door.

Even Gunnar suddenly seemed suspicious in my eyes. He could have framed Zach for the murder, I thought. Perhaps he had gone to the alley that night not to spy on Zach but to gather more evidence to make him look guilty.

It was a stupid thought, and I recognized that I was acting paranoid. It only got worse once the Sanctuary opened at eight o'clock, and I was posted at the front door, tearing tickets and welcoming people. The Saturday night crowd was even bigger than I had imagined, and every guest who walked past me felt threatening. I would jump if anyone made a sudden movement near me, and I was pressed up against the propped-open door so hard I expected to leave a body-shaped impression in the old wood.

When Clara showed up halfway through my shift, I had expected her to simply relieve me for a break. Instead, she told me she was taking my spot for the rest of the night. "There's an electrical issue in the hallway right before the hospital scene," she explained, "so the lights aren't all working. I can't see well at all in the dark, so I thought you might want to stand in there and make sure no one trips or bumps into the props."

I jumped at the offer. I could hide out in a dark corner, where most of the guests wouldn't even see me. It seemed like a safer option than standing right at the front of the Sanctuary, where anyone could find me and target me.

I bumbled my way through the employee hallways between vignettes—I was starting to think of the corridors as tunnels, since they were so narrow and dark—until I finally came out at the hospital scene. The door there had been cleverly disguised to look like the entrance to a morgue. I peeked out and waited for a gap between guests, then I shot out and made a dash for the hallway leading back toward the lagoon vignette. I had to pause and let my eyes adjust because it was so dark. No wonder Clara wanted someone there to help guests along. There was a small recess along the hallway, and I positioned myself in such a way that I could peek at people walking toward me.

It was only after I had stood there for about half an hour that I realized the flaw in my logic. Sure, most guests passed right by me without even suspecting I was there, but if anyone knew where I was, this would be the time and place to come after me. I was alone in the dark.

By the time the last guests of the night had gone past and the overhead lights came on, I was an absolute nervous wreck. My hands were shaking as I pulled my purse out of my locker.

I did exactly as Mama had instructed, making a beeline for the ticket window once I had my things. As soon as I walked out the front doors, though, I saw Damien standing at the window, talking to Zach, and I froze. I did not want to deal with Damien's attitude, and I certainly didn't want to go make conversation with either one of them. Instead, I stood just in front of the doors. I was only a few feet away from the ticket window, so I was in a safe spot.

Zach caught my eye and gave me a wave. I smiled as best as I could amid my nervousness and waved back, right as Damien turned around. He took off his sunglasses and looked at me impatiently. "What are you doing over there?"

"I'm waiting for someone."

"Yeah. Me. I'm staying with you tonight."

CHAPTER TWENTY-TWO

Oh, boy. Mama and I were going to have a long heart-to-heart the next morning. If, that was, I survived spending a night with Damien. I had thought I trusted Mama's judgment, and here she had chosen a possible murderer for my security detail. Had it never occurred to her that Damien could be the one who had left the note telling me to leave town?

No, it hadn't. Of course it hadn't. Mama had been the one who had asked me to go easy on Damien. She seemed to feel sorry for him.

I realized Damien was staring at me, waiting for me to either move or answer him. "It's really not necessary," I said hastily. "I'm sure I'll be fine on my own tonight."

In response, Damien simply crossed his arms.

"I'm sorry you were waiting around for nothing," I continued. "I'll head on out. Um, bye." I pointed myself toward the road and started moving in that direction.

I don't know how Damien closed the space between us so quickly, but suddenly, he was standing right next to me. He pivoted toward me and put his arm out, keeping me from moving forward. I stopped but kept my eyes straight ahead. "I promised Mama," he said. His voice was quiet, but there was no mistaking the authority in his tone. Damien's message was clear: he had agreed to keep an eye on me, and no amount of arguing was going to make him change his mind.

"Fine," I said petulantly.

Damien kept his arm up, extending a finger to point toward the parking lot. "My car is over there."

I let Damien steer me toward a shiny silver Corvette, because of course that was what he was driving while wearing his sunglasses at night. A quick glance showed me that, in fact, he hadn't put them back on. At least I didn't have to worry that he wouldn't be able to see the dark road during the short drive back to the motel.

Neither one of us spoke during the drive, and it wasn't the pleasant kind of silence I had experienced with Zach during the UFO watch party. This was the weird kind of silence that left me thinking about what *he* might be thinking about. It gave me flashbacks to a horrible blind date I had gone on in college. More than two decades was not enough time to forget how terrible of a job my best friend had done playing matchmaker.

I finally opened my mouth again as I unlocked the front door of my apartment and waved Damien inside. "Sorry it's so bare in here. I just got the place today, and I haven't settled in yet." That made it sound like I had a truckload of furniture and belongings waiting to be moved in, but I didn't bother to correct myself. Besides, why was I apologizing for the state of my apartment? I had given Damien every chance not to be my bodyguard, and I certainly wasn't trying to impress the guy.

There weren't any dishes in the kitchen cupboards, so I couldn't even offer Damien a drink of water. I began rummaging through my purse while Damien sat gingerly on the loveseat, his eyes roving around the space disapprovingly. Finally, I pulled out a handful of quarters. "I can go get us sodas out of the vending machine," I said. "What do you want?"

Damien raised one eyebrow. "Do you really think I'd let you do that by yourself? We'll go together."

A few minutes later, Damien was again sitting on the loveseat in a way that said he thought it might dirty up his rear end, but this time, he was doing it with a soda in hand. I plopped down on the foot of my bed and slid my shoes off with my free hand. "So," I began.

"So."

"I don't have a TV yet…"

"We can just talk, then."

Oh, yeah, because that's what I wanted to do. Still, I had wanted an opportunity to ask Damien about his past with both Zach and Jared, and I doubted I would get a better one than this. I had just mustered enough courage to dive in when there was a knock on the door. I tensed up, immediately worried.

Damien rolled his eyes as he rose. "An intruder wouldn't knock first." He opened the door just a crack, then smiled—yes, he could actually smile—and opened the door wide. "Hey, Mama, come on in. You need some help with that?"

It was amazing how Damien's entire demeanor had suddenly changed. He instantly became softer, his face taking on a warmth I hadn't seen in it before and his shoulders relaxing. Even his tone was friendlier.

"I managed to drag it up the stairs, but you can bring it on in," Mama said, jerking her thumb over her shoulder. She stepped past Damien while giving him a pat on the arm. "And how are you holding up, Olivia?"

I shrugged. "Feeling a little paranoid," I said honestly.

"That's understandable. At least you've got Damien to watch over you." Damien was eyeing the rollaway bed he had just hauled through the door, and she said apologetically, "Sorry, kid, it's all I've got."

Mama grinned at me when Damien turned his back to

unfold the rollaway. "It'll be good for him," she whispered. "Get him off his high horse."

I pressed my hand to my mouth to keep from laughing out loud. Mama's trust in him might have been misguided, but at least she recognized that Damien's attitude could stand to be knocked down a notch or two.

Mama yawned. "It's awfully late for me to be up, but I wanted to make sure you two got here safely. I'm going home to bed. Sleep tight, you two."

I followed Mama out the door, shutting it behind me. "He might be the one who left the note," I said quietly.

Mama shook her head. "No. I don't think so. He doesn't give me that vibe."

Great. There's a murderer on the loose and someone threatening me, and Mama is talking about vibes. I widened my eyes, silently pleading with her not to leave me alone with Damien, but she just squeezed my arm reassuringly. "I would know if Damien were hiding a secret that big," she said. "You'll be safe with him. I promise."

Without waiting for me to respond, Mama turned and started heading down the stairs. I considered not even going back inside my apartment. I didn't have the keys to the Caddy on me, which meant I couldn't drive anywhere, but I could go back to the Sanctuary. Or, maybe, I could run to Under the Undertaker's. The supernatural beings there would probably be willing to keep me safe. Unless, of course, the one who had left the note was at the bar, too. My mind sorted through a long list of terrible ideas before I landed on the one that made the most sense.

I should have just asked to spend the night at Mama's house. At the moment, she was the only person in all of Nightmare that I trusted.

"Mama!" I called, hurrying down a few steps. She had just reached the bottom of the stairs, and she was only a few feet from her car.

I heard the door behind me. "Goodnight, Mama. Be safe." Damien's hand curled around my bicep. "Come on, Olivia. Don't stay out here and make yourself a target."

"It's pointless for you to stay," I said. "I'll just catch a ride with Mama back to her house. You can sleep in a real bed, and you don't have to babysit me."

Damien let go of my arm and looked at me like I was a stubborn child. "Don't you think Mama considered that option? Between the two of us, I'm the one who's better able to protect you. Plus, if you're with her, you're putting her in danger, too."

Darn. He has a point.

Reluctantly, I followed Damien inside. The sound of him shutting the door and turning the deadbolt was ominous, the metal clang echoing through my mostly empty apartment.

"I'm going to bed," I said. I grabbed my pajamas out of a dresser drawer and stomped into the bathroom to change. Then I stomped over to the bed and slid under the covers.

Damien did not get the hint. He was sitting on the loveseat again, staring down at his hands. "Olivia," he said, "we still need to talk."

"We don't need to," I argued. "You just suggested it as a way to pass the time."

Damien looked up at me, his green eyes practically shining. It was unnerving, almost unnatural. "Do you still have the job listing you found on the board at the Chamber of Commerce?"

I scrunched up my forehead in confusion. "Yeah, it's over on the kitchen counter, in that pile of papers."

Damien got up and walked to the counter, and as he began to shuffle through the papers, I said sarcastically, "Oh, it's fine. You can just go through all my personal papers without asking first."

When Damien turned to me, he had the listing in his hand. I sat up and pressed my back against the headboard as he walked over to me and sat down on the edge of the bed. He stared at the job listing for a moment, then thrust it toward me. "Do you recognize this handwriting?"

"No, of course I don't." What was he getting at?

"It was written with a fountain pen. You can tell by the unevenness of the ink in some places. And this is my father's handwriting."

I plucked the piece of paper out of Damien's hand and examined it more closely. He was right about the ink. Unlike a modern ball-point pen, the pen that had been used to write the job listing hadn't laid down a steady stream of ink. There was also a light ink splatter in one corner. "Didn't Baxter go missing six months ago?" I asked. "I find it hard to believe this job was posted that long ago, or longer. Surely someone would have filled the position by now."

"Yes, it has been six months," Damien answered stiffly. "And no, this job was not posted that long ago. In fact, it was never posted."

I shook my head. "Yes, it was. I found it on the job board."

"No, Olivia. I talked to Justine. Nightmare didn't have any vacant positions. No one who works there tacked this up on the job board."

"But… How… Did someone think it would be funny to advertise for a job that didn't exist? And if there was no job, then why did Justine give me one?" I pulled my knees up to my chest and wrapped my arms around them. More to myself than to Damien, I said, "This explains why Justine seemed so weird about it when I called."

"You needed a job, and one that didn't even exist magically appeared for you on the job board. And you wonder why Justine gave you the job?"

I laughed. "What, are you implying that I wished the job into existence?"

"Yes."

"Right. I'm secretly a supernatural creature in need of work and protection at the Sanctuary. I manifested the job with my superpowers."

"That's exactly what I think."

CHAPTER TWENTY-THREE

Damien wasn't laughing. My own laugh trailed off, and I fell silent. I shook my head sadly. "Like I've already told you, I'm divorced and broke," I said. "If I had some kind of ability to wish for something, and it would just happen, don't you think I'd be on a yacht in the tropics right now? I wouldn't be living in a one-room apartment at an old motel thanks to the charity of someone who I just met a week ago."

"Maybe you're developing the ability late in life. It's possible that you've always had it, but you're only now tapping into it. It's actually quite interesting. I've heard of conjurors, but I've never met one before."

"Is that what you think I am? A... conjuror?"

"Maybe."

I shook my head again, a lot harder this time. "No. No way. I'm not anything special, and I'm definitely not super-natural." Even while I spoke, I heard Zach and Mori in my head, telling me I belonged at the Sanctuary. I had been scared all night long, but this was another kind of fear alto-gether. I didn't want to be different. I just wanted a normal life again, one that involved having a halfway-decent balance in my checking account and my bare feet on a beach in California.

Eager to shift the focus from me to Damien, I asked, "What kind of supernatural creature are you? You look human, but you must have some unusual ability."

Damien turned his head away from me. Just when I had given up on getting an answer out of him, he mumbled, "I had the ability to get the hell out of this town."

"Why did you come back, when you obviously hate the Sanctuary so much?"

Damien shifted uncomfortably. "I don't hate it." He finally looked at me again, and there was a mixture of sadness and bitterness as he said, "Nightmare Sanctuary is my father's legacy. That makes it my responsibility."

"Was Zach your responsibility, too, back when you were teenagers?" I asked quietly.

I had thought Damien's eyes looked like they were glowing before, but this time, they seemed to flash a brilliant, blinding green. It was so quick I must have imagined it, and I blinked hard a few times. No, I told myself, he just had normal eyes. Good-looking ones, but normal.

"Jared was awful to Zach." I could sense the anger radiating off Damien. Even after all these years, it was obvious he still held a grudge. "He didn't know Zach was a werewolf, of course, but everyone could tell Zach was an awkward guy who didn't fit in with the regular kids. I knew Jared was bullying Zach, but I didn't think it was anything more than teasing. The night I saw Jared and his friends ganging up on Zach, I really thought they were going to kill him."

"And your intervention ended your friendship with Jared?"

"Yeah. I had finally chosen a side, and it was the Sanctuary's. Jared had enjoyed helping us build sets and picking up some cash working for my dad on busy nights. After that, though, he became like everyone else in Nightmare, saying we were all a bunch of freaks who didn't belong here."

"Is that why you left Nightmare after graduation?"

Damien gave me just the hint of a smile. "You've been doing your homework on me, I see. Yes, it's one of the reasons I left. I was never going to have a normal life here. Jared's family has been a part of the community for years, and people would rather listen to his gossip than give me a chance to prove myself."

"Did you kill Jared?" The question popped out of my mouth so unexpectedly I gasped and pressed both hands to my face.

Damien didn't seem at all surprised by my question, which meant he knew that he had a spot on my suspect list. "No. I didn't come to town until I heard about Jared's death. And I don't think Zach killed him, either. He's just not that kind of person."

"Werewolf," I corrected. "And maybe Zach wasn't like that when you were teenagers, but don't forget, he came back here after college. He's had twenty years of being the outcast. I don't want to think Zach killed Jared, either. He even has an alibi for part of that day. Zach told me he was with Jared's widow, Laurie, when the murder happened—"

"What?"

I briefly explained Zach's freelance work as an accountant, and Damien looked angry. "That was stupid of him," he said. "If Jared hadn't been killed, he would have eventually found out. He would have reacted really badly to knowing Zach was the one bailing the ranch out of financial ruin."

"But Jared was killed, so that's a moot point. Like I said, I don't want to think Zach is our killer, either, but we can't count him out. Not yet."

And, I said silently to myself, *we can't count you out, either. You're still on the list.*

There just wasn't much to say after that, and when I yawned widely, Damien stood up. "Try to get some sleep," he said. "You'll be safe tonight."

Strangely, I trusted Damien completely when he said that. I didn't know what tomorrow would bring, but I believed that I was at least going to make it to daybreak. Dangerous or not, Damien had a promise to keep. I scooted down in bed, curled up in a ball, and fell asleep before Damien had even turned the light off.

I woke up a lot during the night, thanks to crazy dreams that involved me getting hundreds of notes under my door and shadowy figures chasing me down the street. Every time I sat up gasping, I could see Damien. He had positioned the rollaway bed right in front of the door, and he was sitting up against it, still awake. His eyes glinted in the glow of the moonlight coming through the windows. Eventually, I decided his supernatural power was the ability to go without sleep.

It was knocking on the door that finally woke me up for good, and I was mildly surprised to see it was full daylight out. At some point, my exhaustion had finally gotten the upper hand against my bad dreams, and I had enjoyed a long chunk of uninterrupted sleep. The clock on the nightstand read nine o'clock as I watched Damien move the rollaway and answer the door.

Mama had brought us coffee and donuts, which we both gratefully accepted. She joined us at the square Formica table, which sat in front of the kitchenette, and we reported that it had been a quiet night. "What are your plans for today?" she asked me before taking a huge bite of a chocolate-glazed donut.

In addition to the bad dreams, my subconscious had

also been hatching a plan while I'd slept. "Actually, I'd like to talk to Emmett today."

Damien stiffened. "I'm not sure that's a good idea."

"Why not?"

He held up one finger. "For one thing, you've already been threatened, and it could be dangerous if you're so obviously continuing to look for Jared's killer." Damien held up a second finger. "For another, what if Emmett *is* the killer?"

"I'm going to visit his office, not some secret location in a remote area. I should be perfectly safe."

Damien shook his head. "Even if Emmett isn't guilty, he's not someone whose bad side you want to be on."

"Like Jared was?" I asked, raising an eyebrow.

"And my father. I know I said Dad would turn up eventually, but I'm honestly worried. He would never abandon the Sanctuary. Those people are his family." Damien raised his coffee cup, and just before his lips touched the rim, he mumbled, "More than I ever was."

"You think Emmett might have had something to do with your dad's disappearance, like everyone else at the Sanctuary believes."

"I do."

"All the more reason for me to have a chat with him, then." I refused to be deterred. Some little tickle in my brain was telling me it was time to confront the real estate agent, whose name kept coming up in all of this. "If you don't think it's safe, then do you want to tag along as my bodyguard?"

"That would be the safer option, but I doubt you'd get any information out of him if I was there. I don't like the idea of you confronting Emmett, but I'm not going to stop you."

Mama had been watching our exchange silently, the donut in her hand entirely forgotten for the moment.

Finally, she said, "Stick to the busy streets, ask questions but don't fling accusations, and report to me the second you get back."

I gave Mama a little salute. Clearly, she had already figured out that I could be stubborn, and she knew there was no point in trying to change my mind. I appreciated that.

Soon, Mama said she had to get back to the front office, and Damien took that as his cue to leave, too. I thanked him profusely as he walked out the door. I still thought he was a jerk, and I still thought he might have had something to do with Jared's murder—my current motto was *Don't trust anybody*—but if it hadn't been for his overnight vigil, I doubted I would have slept at all.

Damien had told me where to find Emmett's office, and I was pleased to learn it was just one block down from the Lusty Lunch Counter. I could reward myself with a cheeseburger afterward.

Not only did I stick to the busiest streets on my trip over to Emmett's office, but I drove instead of walking. It was nice to arrive somewhere without a layer of sweat over my face, and I definitely felt safer.

Emmett's office was a simple glass-fronted space in a long, low adobe building that was faintly pink in color. There were printouts of houses and land for sale taped in the office's front windows, nearly blocking the view inside. The sign on the door read *Closed*, but I took a chance and knocked anyway. I wasn't willing to give up just yet.

When my knuckles hit the door, it jiggled slightly in the frame. I pushed my palm against it, and it opened for me. I found it strange that the front door was unlocked when the office was supposed to be closed, and I stepped over the threshold cautiously.

The office looked completely normal, but no one was inside. I walked up to the wide desk at the back of the office, thinking I could leave a note asking Emmett to call me. As I got closer, I could see there was a sheet of paper lying right in the middle of the desk. *Stop asking* had been written on it in large letters.

The handwriting was exactly the same as the warning note that had been shoved under my front door.

CHAPTER TWENTY-FOUR

I froze, my eyes fixed on the note. It was obvious whoever had threatened me had written this note, too. That left a very important question, though. Were Emmett and I being threatened by the same person, or had Emmett written both notes? After all, this one was sitting right in the middle of his desk. I realized with a start that Emmett had probably written this note with the intention of giving it to me since I obviously hadn't left town. He was planning to give me another nudge to mind my own business.

I spun on my heel and sprinted toward the front door. Just as I reached it, the door opened, and I stopped short as I recognized Emmett right in front of me.

Emmett jumped and pressed a hand over his heart, his eyes staring at me wildly. He seemed more upset to see me than I was to see him. He stood there in the doorway, breathing hard. "You're the one who found Jared."

I nodded, too scared for any words to actually come out of my mouth.

"Did you do it?" he asked breathlessly.

That accusation startled me into talking. "Did I... kill Jared?"

"No. Did you leave that note?"

"Me? No. I thought maybe you were the one who had left a note for me."

"You got one, too?"

"It was a different message, but it was still a warning. In that same handwriting."

Emmett glanced quickly in both directions, peering down the sidewalk before looking at me again. "Someone shoved it under my door just a few minutes ago. I ran around the block to see if I could find who did it." He was so frazzled I began to believe he really was on the receiving end of the note, rather than being its author.

"Let's talk," I suggested.

"Not here," Emmett said hastily. He ran a hand through his hair. "Somewhere public, where there are other people."

"How about an early lunch, then? My treat." I couldn't really afford to be buying someone lunch, but if it meant I might get some valuable information out of Emmett, then it would be worth the expense.

Emmett locked up his office, then we made the short walk to the Lusty Lunch Counter. I waved at Ella, who was behind the counter, but instead of heading for my usual stool, Emmett and I chose a booth in the far back corner. It was too early for the lunch crowd, and the booth was far enough from the other diners that we could talk freely without being overheard.

"The note is about Jared, then," Emmett said. He pulled a white handkerchief out of his pocket and wiped his brow. "I've heard you're looking into his murder. If you got a similar note, then that's the only thing that makes sense."

"The note on your desk read *Stop asking*. That implies you've been doing some investigating, too."

"I haven't, though. I want to know who killed Jared, of course. He wasn't exactly a friend, but we've known each other for years, and he was a good guy. But I wasn't going

160

around asking questions or trying to find out who did it. I'm perfectly happy to leave that up to the police."

I cleared my throat and said, as politely as possible, "You realize that you're also a suspect, right?"

Emmett wiped his brow again. A server came over right then to take our drink orders, and he asked for an iced tea in a shaky voice. Once we were alone again, he leaned across the table and hissed, "Of course I know that! An officer came to my house the night Jared was found. Someone tipped them off that he and I had been arguing here at the diner."

That had been me, but I wasn't about to admit it to Emmett. "And what did you tell the police?"

"What could I tell them? I was out looking at property east of town, by myself, the day Jared died. I have no alibi to prove I didn't do it. Then again, there's nothing to prove I did. I've got a good reputation in this town, so I'm confident I'll come out of this just fine."

I resisted the urge to tell Emmett he certainly didn't look or sound confident.

I thought back to what others had said about Emmett. His reputation seemed to be that he could be a ruthless real estate agent, and it was wise not to cross him in business dealings. Either Emmett was lying about his reputation, or there were people in Nightmare who didn't mind his tactics.

I also reminded myself that, as Mori had told me, there were different Nightmares. The supernatural community might view Emmett as dangerous, but the rest of the town might not.

"Of course," Emmett continued once we had our drinks in front of us, "everyone knows Laurie wanted Jared to sell the ranch. I pretty much had him talked into it, since I upped my offer shortly after our argument here at the diner. Of course, now that he's dead, Laurie and I can make a deal, though I'm fully aware it will only make me look more suspicious in the eyes of some folks." Emmett stopped talking to gulp down half of his iced tea. He stared down into it as he said slowly, "Maybe she did it."

"I've considered that. Laurie knew the ranch was in financial trouble, and she wanted Jared to agree to the sale. It's possible she killed her own husband." I kept my voice low, not wanting anyone to overhear me talking so blatantly about Laurie. Even while I was laying out the possibility of Laurie's guilt, I reminded myself that Emmett could still be the one who had killed Jared. Perhaps he really had written the note I found on his desk, only so he could pretend to be an innocent victim in all of this. His nervousness seemed real, but it could be solely because I was getting closer to the truth.

I barely touched my cheeseburger when it arrived. I was too nervous to eat. Emmett, on the other hand, chowed down on a roast beef sandwich like he hadn't eaten in days.

Once we finished eating, I paid and rose to leave. I was just about to thank Emmett for his time when he said, "If you come back to the office with me, there's something else I want you to see."

My guard instantly went up. If there was more evidence, then why hadn't Emmett mentioned it yet? Going back to his office might mean I was walking into a trap. For better or for worse, my curiosity and my stubbornness to solve this murder outweighed the danger signals my brain was sending out. I agreed, and we walked back to the office. I kept an eye on Emmett, and I slowly snuck my hand into my purse to pull out the keys to the Caddy. Not to escape, but to defend myself. It was the closest thing I had to a weapon.

Emmett unlocked the door, and when he waved me in, I paused. "No, you go first. I'll follow," I said. He just shrugged and complied, and once we were inside, I kept my back up against the door. I wanted the easiest escape route possible.

"Hang on," Emmett said. He seemed oblivious to my cautious stance.

Emmett rummaged around in the bottom drawer of a filing cabinet before returning his attention to me. He muttered an *oh* of surprise when he saw I was still at the door, and he closed the space between us so he could hand me a manilla file folder.

I shoved my car key into the pocket of my shorts and accepted the folder. Inside were four aerial photos of a hilly landscape. I flipped through them quickly, but nothing about them seemed like a clue to a murder. "What are these?" I asked.

"These are satellite images of Barker Ranch," Emmett said. He pointed at a dark spot on the photo sitting on the top. "See that? It's the opening to a mine shaft."

"How is that significant to Jared's murder?"

"Nightmare only exists because of the copper mine. It gave up its last ore years ago, but there are dozens of smaller mines in this area. Some aren't any more than ground tests that failed to show promising signs. Others have a fair number of tunnels that yielded a decent amount of copper."

"Surely there's nothing left to find, though," I said.

"Maybe there's no copper to find, but mines around here can still hold value. Crystals, minerals, even gold."

"Did Jared know there was a mine on his property?"

Emmett shrugged. "He did, but he told me he didn't see any value in it. It's not in a place that's easy to reach, so he ignored it."

"Then why did he bother to tell you about it?" I asked.

There was no sign of embarrassment or shame in Emmett's expression as he answered, "He didn't. Barker

Ranch is on a valuable spot of land for the view alone. I started looking at satellite images to see how luxury cabins could be arranged on the land, and I spotted the mine. Out here, seeing an old mine on a plot of land is no surprise. When I asked Jared about it, he said he knew it existed, but he had never cared to seek it out."

"I feel like there's a 'but' coming."

"Take a closer look at the rest of the photos."

I did as Emmett instructed, but for the life of me, I couldn't see anything different from the first photo, except that one image was greener than the others and had clearly been taken during a rainier time of year.

When I continued to stare blankly at the photos, Emmett pointed at the second one. "Look at the area around the mine."

I squinted. It was tiny, but I could see there was a car parked not far from the mine. I flipped to the third and fourth photos, and the same car was there in each one. I gasped. "Someone has been visiting the mine."

"Exactly. I don't know who, and I don't know for what, but there is, apparently, something of value in that mine."

I looked up from the photo I was studying. "You didn't want Barker Ranch just so you could build luxury cabins on it, did you? And I'm guessing you never told Jared your suspicions about the mine's worth."

"You can imagine why I haven't shared this information with the police. It would make me look really bad."

"Then why are you telling me? I could just go to the police and tip them off."

Emmett's mouth twisted. "I'm trusting you not to. If you're getting threatening notes under your door, then you're close to finding the truth. I'm hoping this information might help you."

"Thanks. But I have one question. If a car has been driving this close to the mine, then obviously there's a road.

You can even see that the car is parked at the end of what looks like a dirt lane. Why haven't you gone to the mine to explore it yourself?"

"I've tried, but I can't figure out where the road begins. Its entrance is hidden by a hill or plants, or something, and trying to cut through the vegetation on foot is practically impossible. The steep angle of the hills around the mine and the high concentration of cacti make a great natural barrier."

"It's too bad there's not more detail in this photo. The car seems to be a dark color, but that's really all I can tell. Still, this could be useful info, like you said. Thanks, Emmett."

"Good luck."

I said goodbye to Emmett, but as I did so, my eyes flicked past him. There was a calendar on the wall behind his desk, and I saw Emmett had a meeting scheduled for Monday. In red ink, he had written, *Damien, 2:00.*

CHAPTER TWENTY-FIVE

My brain was racing in a hundred different directions as I walked out of Emmett's office. Not only did I have this secret mine to consider, but now I had to worry even more that Damien really was going to sell the Sanctuary to Emmett.

Any of the pleasant things I had thought about Damien—him defending Zach when they were teenagers, him dutifully watching over me all night—were overshadowed by his apparent eagerness to ruin the lives of everyone working at the haunt. I caught myself muttering under my breath as I made the short drive back to the motel.

I did exactly as promised, stopping at the office to check in with Mama before returning to my apartment. I didn't tell her about the mine or Emmett's own threatening note, but I did assure her that we had discussed things civilly and in a public setting.

"Good. I'm glad you're being careful. We just got you, Olivia, and we don't want to lose you so soon." Mama smiled. "I'm sure Damien would like another chance to play hero for you."

"I'm sure," I said sarcastically. After what I had spied on Emmett's calendar, Damien had moved to the top of the suspect list again. Finding a body at the Sanctuary would be the perfect excuse for him to sell the place, take his money, and run as far from Nightmare as he could.

"Good riddance," I said out loud.

"What's that?" Mama asked.

"Oh, nothing. Just… talking to myself."

"Before you go, take this." Mama produced a little flip phone and held it out toward me. "It's Lucy's. She left it here, and you need it more than her right now. My number is in there, and I programmed Damien's in, too. But if things go really bad, you call the police."

"I will. Thanks for looking out for me, Mama."

Mama clucked her tongue, but she was smiling. "Someone has to."

When I got back to my apartment, I immediately sat down at the table with a pen and the warning note. I flipped it over so I could write on the backside. I made a list of everyone who was still on my suspect list, no matter how unlikely they might seem: Damien, Laurie, and Emmett were on the non-supernatural list, and I put Zach and Mori on the list for Sanctuary suspects.

Of all of them, I thought Damien and Laurie would be the ones most likely to know about the mine. I didn't want to deal with Damien at the moment. I was too angry with him, and I figured I would do more yelling than questioning if I confronted him now. That left Laurie.

The drive to Barker Ranch seemed to take ages because I was so anxious to get more answers. Finally, I arrived, and I drove right up to the front of the house. I jumped out and rang the doorbell, but no one answered. I rang again, then knocked a few times, but still, there was no answer.

There was a car in the driveway, so Laurie had to be home. The logical side of my brain told me she must be in the shower or taking a nap, but at the same time, I worried something bad had happened to her, too. I made a quick lap around the house, hoping I would see her on the back porch or out working in a flower bed, but no one was there.

Feeling panic welling up inside me, I turned in a full circle once I was in the front yard again. The only other likely spot for Laurie to be was the barn, so I hurried in that direction. By the time I neared the wooden door, I was running.

I wrenched the barn door open. The rusted hinges squealed loudly, so if Laurie was inside, she would definitely know she had a visitor.

But Laurie wasn't in there. The barn was empty. I even looked behind a rusty old tractor and a pile of storage boxes, in case she was crouched behind them, but I had the place all to myself.

Once my quick search was finished, I stood in the center of the barn and wondered where else I could look. My gut was telling me something bad had happened to her and that I needed to hurry. As I thought, I stared at the wall in front of me, not really seeing what was there at first. Slowly, I became aware that I was looking at a row of soil aerators hanging from iron hooks on the wall. Each one had five sharp metal tines at the end, made for punching into the hard Arizona dirt.

The tines looked an awful lot like claws, and one of the hooks stood empty.

Zach hadn't killed Jared. Someone without any supernatural abilities had killed him, using the aerator to simulate claw marks. I instinctively knew I was right.

Maybe Laurie wasn't missing because someone had come after her. Perhaps she had gone into hiding because she was guilty.

But there was another person who was even more of a

likely killer than Laurie. I should have realized it as soon as I saw the aerial photos, but the claw marks on Jared's body were the one thing that kept throwing me off. I had been trying to put a puzzle together in my mind for the past week, and now that I knew the claw marks had been faked, the pieces suddenly fit together.

And if I was right, then Laurie really was in danger. I prayed it wasn't too late for her as I sprinted out of the barn.

I rounded the corner of the barn and immediately ducked back. A black car was rolling along the dirt driveway, but it was coming from the direction of the house.

No, I realized. Laurie's car had been the only one parked at the house, and it was red. This car was coming from the hidden path that led to the mine. It had to be, because where else could it have been completely hidden from me as I had run around the house?

I peeked around the corner of the barn as the car got closer, and I knew it had to be the same car I had seen in the aerial photos. I had seen it a couple other times, too.

I turned and pressed my back against the side of the barn, listening to the sound of the car's tires against the dirt road. I waited anxiously for the car to pass, and my heart leaped wildly when the sound suddenly ceased.

Then I heard a car door open and close, followed by the dull thud of someone vaulting over the fence. Luke Dawes, the man who had killed Jared Barker, was walking right toward me. Luke must have seen my car up at the house and known I was snooping around. I was almost certain he was looking for me.

Had he seen me? I had nowhere to go but back into the barn. I moved as quietly as I could, but there was no way to keep those rusty door hinges from squeaking. I slid inside, leaving the door ajar, and wedged myself behind the tractor. Dirt and old hay dust puffed up when I crouched down, and I pinched my nose to keep from sneezing.

I pulled Lucy's cell phone out of my pocket. Luke would hear me if I called the police. Instead, I texted both Mama and Damien. I kept the text short, telling them I was in danger at Barker Ranch and to call the police. I hoped one of them would see the message in time.

I berated myself for not having realized the truth sooner. Luke was the only person other than Jared and Laurie who had full access to Barker Ranch. Not only was Luke out there at night for his UFO watch parties, but he was even out there during the day to tend to his moonflower crop. I had to wonder if he even believed in UFOs, or if the whole thing was just a charade so he had an excuse to be on the property.

On Friday night, I had been sitting right next to Luke at the watch party, where Zach and I had discussed the murder case. We had kept our voices low, but it would have been easy enough for Luke to eavesdrop. My interest in finding Jared's killer had probably put Luke on his guard, and he had slipped that note under my door to warn me off.

Even the note Emmett had gotten made sense now. *Stop asking* had nothing to do with asking questions about Jared's murder. Instead, Luke wanted Emmett to stop asking to buy Barker Ranch. If the whole place was developed, Luke would lose access to the mine and whatever value he had found in it.

I crouched behind the tractor for so long my knees began to protest. Maybe, I told myself, Luke had turned around and gone back to his car. Or, my brain argued, maybe he was standing outside the barn, waiting to catch me on my way out.

I guess he got tired of waiting, because just as I was thinking about standing up to stretch my legs, the barn door groaned, and I heard soft footsteps. My breath seemed loud in my ears, but not loud enough to cover the soft sound of scraping and the *clink* of metal. Luke had taken an aerator off the wall.

Luke's footsteps sounded quietly through the barn, and eventually, they got louder as he approached my hiding place. I held my breath and hoped he wouldn't look behind the tractor.

I heard a low laugh, then Luke said, "I know you're back there, Olivia."

Feeling utterly trapped, I jumped up and moved out of my hiding place, but I kept the tractor between Luke and me. He held the aerator loosely in his hands, but his wild eyes and grim smile told me he fully intended to use it on me.

Running would do nothing for me. Luke would tackle me long before I made it to the barn door. Instead, I tried to distract him. "How did you know about Zach?" I asked.

My plan worked, a least for a few seconds. Luke paused and gave me a confused look. "Know what about Zach?"

"The aerator," I said, jerking my chin toward the one in Luke's hands. "You used one on Jared to make it look like he'd been clawed."

"What does that have to do with Zach?"

"You killed Jared, then made it look like he'd been attacked by a creature with claws and dumped the body at the Sanctuary," I prompted. "You framed Zach perfectly."

"I added the marks to make it look like Jared had been attacked by the same thing that killed his cows. They had claw marks on them, too. Of course, I couldn't drain his blood to exactly match the cows, but I figured someone would make the connection."

I was so surprised that I forgot to be afraid for a second. Luke had been trying to frame the chupacabra, and he had inadvertently made Zach look guilty. "Then why did you leave Jared's body at the Sanctuary?" I asked.

"I knew the police wouldn't be happy with the explanation that Jared had been killed by a mysterious animal no one had ever seen. They could take their pick of the freaks at the Sanctuary instead. And I'm done talking. Let's get down to more important business."

Luke began to move toward the front of the tractor. I remembered there was a side door, which was behind me. I would have a better chance of getting through it than the big door at the front. It took every ounce of courage I had to turn my back on Luke, but I did, and I ran as fast as I could to the side door. Thankfully, it wasn't locked, and I dashed out of it.

I threw a glance over my shoulder as I neared the driveway. Luke was nearly in striking distance. There was nothing I could do but keep running. I scrambled over the low wooden fence, and then I started laughing. A police car was coming up the driveway, right toward me. I waved my arms and headed toward the car as it skidded to a stop.

Luke dropped the aerator and ran back toward the barn as two officers leaped out of the car. Finally feeling safe, I was happy to watch the show. In short order, Luke was in handcuffs.

The sound of more cars made me turn around, and I saw a minivan and an SUV coming to a stop behind the police car. A few people I didn't know got out, and then I saw Laurie emerge from the passenger side of the minivan.

Relief flooded through me, even as I shook my head at my totally misplaced panic about Laurie's safety. I had forgotten she had family in town for Jared's funeral. Clearly, they had all gone out, probably to lunch, and they had simply left Laurie's car at the house.

Laurie ran up to me, her eyes wide. "Is Luke being arrested?" she asked incredulously.

By that point, Luke and the officers had nearly reached the patrol car. Luke lunged toward Laurie and me, and the officers gripped him by the arms.

Luke began to shout at Laurie, spit flying from his lips. "It was supposed to be you! I thought it was you walking into the barn that day! If I had gotten rid of you, I could have talked Jared into keeping this land!"

CHAPTER TWENTY-SIX

Before I drove to the police station to give my statement, I checked my phone. Mama and Damien had both texted me back, saying the police had been called and were on their way. Those messages were followed by three more from Mama, asking if I was okay. I responded, thanking both of them for saving my life and promising to give them the full story soon.

Laurie had broken down in hysterics after finding out she had been the intended victim, so it was a good thing she had her family there to support her. By the time I saw her again at the police station, she had calmed down considerably.

I figured the only winner in all of this was Emmett, who would probably buy the ranch without a hitch.

After I told the police everything that had happened, the same officer I had talked to twice already in the past week, Officer Reyes, came in and sat down across from me. I was in someone's office, so at least it felt like a casual conversation rather than an interrogation.

"Silver," he said. "That's what Mr. Dawes found in the mine. Jared had mentioned the ranch had a mine on it somewhere, and Dawes didn't rest until he had found it. There wasn't enough silver to make the mine viable as a commercial operation, but for one man, it equaled some significant extra income. He would extract a little at a time, and he figured he could use the mine as his personal bank for years to come."

"Luke killed Jared over money," I said flatly.

"It's more common than you might think." The officer rose, then extended a hand. "Thank you, Ms. Kendrick. Without your interference, we wouldn't have Jared's killer behind bars right now."

I ignored the "interference" part and graciously shook the officer's hand.

When I got back to the motel, I walked into the office and was nearly tackled by Mama, who caught me up in a fierce hug. I gave her the blow-by-blow account of my experience, and she threw in plenty of *how awfuls* and *what a shames*, as well as a few choice expletives.

After I had finished my story, Mama gave me a searching look. "Nick says your car is ready, and you solved the murder. What are you going to do now?"

I opened my mouth before I realized I just didn't know the answer to her question. Actually, there was one honest response I could give. "I'm going to go to work tonight, and I'm going to feel perfectly safe."

And that's exactly what I did. I walked to the Sanctuary rather than driving that evening. I had taken a hot shower and a long nap after checking in with Mama, and I was feeling refreshed. At the same time, though, I had nervous energy coursing through me. I really didn't know what I wanted to do. My plan had been to hit the road the second Jared's murder had been solved and I had the money for my car. That would mean I would remain in Nightmare for just under one more week. At the moment, though, I wasn't sure I wanted to go to San Diego anymore. All I had wanted when I had left Nashville was to start my life over, and I felt like I was already doing that in Nightmare.

When I crested the hill on the road that led to the Sanctuary and saw the old hospital building in front of me, I actually felt something like satisfaction. Whatever I decided to do, I promised myself I would enjoy my night. I would be as spooky and welcoming as I could be.

When I passed the ticket window, the door flew open, and I saw a blur of movement. Zach threw his arms around me. "We heard what happened," he said. "Thank you."

I hugged him back, even though I was stunned at this show of affection from Mr. Surly himself. Still, by catching Jared's real killer, it meant Zach's name had been cleared, and I could see how that might put him in a rare good mood.

When Zach let me go, he said, "You're wanted in Damien's office. He and I actually had a long talk earlier."

"Good," I said sincerely.

I only felt a little trepidation as I headed down the hall to Damien's office. The door was open, so I knocked against the doorframe as I walked in. "You wanted to see me?" I asked.

Damien looked up from the papers he had been perusing, and he breathed out a sigh. "You're safe."

I gestured to myself. "Clearly."

"I wanted to see it for myself, even though you had texted that you were okay." Damien leaned back in his chair. "Congratulations. Not only did you catch a killer, but you also single-handedly saved the Sanctuary. Once again, your wish has become reality. We're staying open."

I plopped down into a chair. "I'm relieved to know you're not closing the Sanctuary, but it wasn't any of this conjuror magic you think I have that's keeping it open. Now everyone knows Luke Dawes killed Jared, not someone at the Sanctuary, so you don't have an excuse to shut us down."

"If I wanted to shut this haunt down, I would just do it. I wouldn't need an excuse," Damien grumbled. *Ah, there it is,* I thought. *He's still a jerk underneath his concern for me.* "Still, I've decided not to give up on the Sanctuary just yet."

"I appreciate it. We all do. But I also know you've got a meeting with Emmett tomorrow."

Damien pursed his lips. "That's my business, not yours. And I mean that literally. If I'm staying in town, I need somewhere to live. Emmett is going to help me find a place. Plus"—Damien lowered his voice—"you know I think Emmett might have had something to do with my dad's disappearance. I want to spend some time with him, maybe ask a few questions to get a feel for what he knows, or what he might have done."

"There's our hero." It was Mori's voice, and I turned to see her standing in the doorway, her grin wide. "I just woke up and got the scoop. I guess I need to go apologize to Zach. But first, I wanted to thank you, Olivia." Felipe wiggled past Mori and scrambled up onto my lap, then began to nuzzle my arm.

"You're welcome," I told Mori.

"Do you know why Justine invited you to go through the haunt as a regular guest before you started your job here?"

"I figured it was some kind of hazing. If I could survive all of you trying to scare me to death, then I could work here."

Mori laughed. "Did I come off as scary? Whoops. Actually, Justine wasn't sure what to make of you. She wanted to get our impressions, too, especially from those with extrasensory abilities. The witches said you gave off a really good energy."

So my trip through the Sanctuary hadn't been hazing, but one giant job interview. I winked at Mori. "I'm glad I passed the test."

"What are you going to do now?" Damien asked.

I turned back to him. "My car is fixed, and now I just need to pay for the repairs."

"And then?"

"Mama asked me the same thing. Honestly, I'm not sure."

"You belong here," Mori said. "We can all see that."

I smiled and scratched Felipe behind one ear. "Maybe I'll stick around for a few weeks. Nightmare isn't so bad, after all."

A NOTE FROM THE AUTHOR

Reader, I hope you're having as much fun as I am in the quirky old mining town of Nightmare. I got the inspiration for this series one October, when I was lamenting that I don't live anywhere close to a year-round haunted house attraction. The next best thing, I decided, was to have a character who not only lived near one, but actually worked there. I'm excited to learn more about the residents—both normal and supernatural—of Nightmare, and to find out what trouble Olivia gets herself into next!

Before you go, would you please leave a review? It means so much to indie authors like me. Thank you for your support!

Eternally Yours,

Beth

P.S. You can keep up with my latest book news, get fun freebies, and more by signing up for my newsletter at http://bethdolgner.com!

Drowning at the Diner

NIGHTMARE, ARIZONA BOOK TWO
PARANORMAL COZY MYSTERIES

Death, Danger, and Dirty Dishes in Nightmare, Arizona.

Her car might be fixed, but that doesn't mean Olivia Kendrick is leaving the town of Nightmare, Arizona just yet. As she settles into her new life working at Nightmare Sanctuary Haunted House, Olivia still wants to know what Damien Shackleford really is, other than handsome, brooding, and a total jerk.

When the new dishwasher at the Lusty Lunch Counter is found drowned in a sink full of dirty dishes, Olivia's friend Ella is the main suspect. After all, the victim had been stalking her. At the same time, the arrival of a mysterious stranger will lead to an astonishing discovery about the diner owner's violent past.

Olivia will enlist the supernatural beings at Nightmare Sanctuary to help her track down the truth and clear her friend's name.

At the same time, Olivia begins to hear a phantom voice from an abandoned mine at the edge of Nightmare, and it seems to be tied to the disappearance of Damien's father. Is Olivia tapping into her own supernatural ability, or is something sinister lurking in the old tunnels…?

ACKNOWLEDGMENTS

Thank you to my test readers Alex, David, Kristine, Lisa, Mom, and Sabrina: I'm so grateful to have you on my team! Jena at BookMojo keeps me sane and sorted, and she came up with gorgeous covers for this series. Lia at Your Best Book Editor and Trish at Blossoming Pages worked editing magic to polish my manuscript.

ACKNOWLEDGEMENTS

ABOUT THE AUTHOR

Beth Dolgner writes paranormal fiction and nonfiction. Her interest in things that go bump in the night really took off on a trip to Savannah, Georgia, so it's fitting that her first series—Betty Boo, Ghost Hunter—takes place in that spooky city. Beth also writes paranormal nonfiction, including her first book, *Georgia Spirits and Specters*, which is a collection of Georgia ghost stories.

Beth and her husband, Ed, live in Tucson, Arizona, with their three cats. They're close enough to Tombstone that Beth can easily visit its Wild West street and watch staged shootouts, all in the name of research for the Nightmare, Arizona series.

Beth also enjoys giving presentations on Victorian death and mourning traditions as well as Victorian Spiritualism. She has been a volunteer at an historic cemetery, a ghost tour guide, and a paranormal investigator.

Keep up with Beth and sign up for her newsletter at BethDolgner.com.

BOOKS BY BETH DOLGNER

The Nightmare, Arizona Series

Paranormal Cozy Mystery

Homicide at the Haunted House

Drowning at the Diner (June 2023)

The Eternal Rest Bed and Breakfast Series

Paranormal Cozy Mystery

Sweet Dreams

Late Checkout

Picture Perfect

Scenic Views

Breakfast Included

Groups Welcome

Quiet Nights

The Betty Boo, Ghost Hunter Series

Romantic Urban Fantasy

Ghost of a Threat

Ghost of a Whisper

Ghost of a Memory

Ghost of a Hope

Manifest

Young Adult Steampunk

A Talent for Death

Young Adult Urban Fantasy

Nonfiction

Georgia Spirits and Specters

Everyday Voodoo